François de Salignac de La Mothe- Fénelon

Ethic Amusements

Ethic tales and fables

François de Salignac de La Mothe- Fénelon

Ethic Amusements
Ethic tales and fables

ISBN/EAN: 9783337175238

Printed in Europe, USA, Canada, Australia, Japan

Cover: Foto ©Andreas Hilbeck / pixelio.de

More available books at **www.hansebooks.com**

BY PERMISSION,

COPIES

OF THE

ETHIC AMUSEMENTS

HAVE BEEN MOST HUMBLY PRESENTED,

TÖ

* THE KING.

* THE QUEEN.

* HIS ROYAL HIGHNESS THE PRINCE OF WALES.

* HER ROYAL HIGHNESS THE PRINCESS DOWAGER OF WALES.

* HIS ROYAL HIGHNESS FREDERICK BISHOP OF OSNABRUG.

*. HIS ROYAL HIGHNESS PRINCE WILLIAM.

SUBSCRIBERS NAMES.

A.

SIR Charles Afgill, Bart.
   Mrs. Amyand
Mrs. Afhers
Mrs. Allen
John Arbuthnot, Efq;
Thomas Adderley, Efq;
John Armitage, Efq;
Mr Henry Andrews
Mr. Hendyn Allen
Mr. Saint Allтом
Mr. Richard Arnott
Mr. Thomas Allen

B.

* The Right Hon. the Earl of Bute
The Right Hon. Lord Vifcount Boling-
   broke
Mrs. Burdett
Mifs Bilcliffe
Mrs. Bacon
Mrs. R. Briflowe
Mrs. Browne, of Strand
Mrs. Brown, of Richmond
Mifs S. Browne
Mrs. Bridges
* Mifs Beal
* Mrs. Bellamy
Mrs. Anne Bellamy
George Baker, M. D. Phyfician to the
   Royal Houfehold, and F. R. S.
* John Baker, M. D. of Richmond.
The Rev George Bellas, D. D.
Richard Belfon, Efq;
Chriftopher Blanchard, Efq;
John Bell, Efq;
—— Briflow, Efq;

William Blair, Efq;
John Briftowe, Efq;
Thomas Burdett, Efq;
Bartholomew Burton, Efq;
* Frederick William Blomberg, Efq;
—— Bayley, Efq;
Nathaniel Bayley, Efq;
James Bonnell, Efq;
James Beal, Efq;
John Bulley, Efq; Writing-mafter to
   the Princes
* The Rev. Mr. John Burrough, Fel-
   low of Magdalen-College, Oxford
The Rev. Mr. Charles Brown
Mr. Henry Bell
Mr. George Bickham
Mr. John Bickham
Mr. Solomon Browne
Mr. Bradbury
* Mr. Thomas Bellamy
* Mr. Thomas Bellamy, Jun.
Mr. Edward Ballard, Bookfeller
Mr. Nathaniel Burrough
* Mr. Boydell, Engraver, two books
* Mrs Baldwin
Mifs Baldwin

C.

* His Grace the Lord Archbifhop of
   Canterbury
* The Right Hon. the Countefs of
   Cowper
* The Right Hon. the Lady Camden
The Hon. Lady Margaret Compton
The Hon Mrs. Clutterbuck
Sir James Cockbourne

                  * The

SUBSCRIBERS NAMES.

* The Rev. John Cofens, D. D. Mini-
ſter of Teddington, and Chaplain
to the Right Hon. the Earl of Den-
bigh
* The Rev. James Carrington, M. A.
Chancellor of Exeter
Mrs. Calliaud
* Mrs. Cotefworth
Mrs. Cutts
Mrs. Curtis
Mrs. Collins, Hill-ſtreet, Richmond
Mrs. Collington
Miſs Crofts
Mrs. Campbell
* Mrs. Cofens
* Miſs Frances Carrington
—— Chambers, Eſq;
* John Cooke, Eſq;
George Carrington, Eſq;
—— Clark, Eſq;
Stephen Cazalet, Eſq;
* Claude Crefpigny, Eſq; LL. D.
* Claude Champion Crefpigny, Eſq;
* Philip Champion Crefpigny, Eſq;
John Chafe, Eſq;
* George Chadd, Eſq;
Edward Collins, Eſq;
—— Crop, Eſq;
Richard Curfon, Eſq;
George Colman, Eſq;
—— Chefter, Eſq;
James Campbell, Eſq;
William Chambers, Eſq; of the Royal
Academy
The Rev. Mr. Collard, Vicar of Twick-
enham
The Rev. Spark Cauham, M. A. Chap-
lain to the Right Hon. the Earl of
Plymouth
The Rev. Mr. James Carrington,
Jun.
Mr. Richard Carpenter
Mr. John Corp   -
Mr. Cliefden

Mr. Samuel Chriſtopher
Meſſ. Curtis, Stationers
Mr. Benj. Cole, Engraver
Mr. Edward Clark

D.

The Right Hon. Lady Delamer
The Rev. Benjamin Dawfon, LL. D.
John D'Urban, M. D.
Mrs. Dubois
Mrs. Delafoſſe
Mrs. Denoyer
Miſs Denoyer
* Miſs Duck
Charles Deaves, Eſq;
James Davis, Eſq; Quarter-maſter,
Light-horfe
—— Dorell, Eſq;
B. Gurdon Dillingham, Eſq;
Abraham de Paibe, Eſq;
Philip Denoyer, Eſq;
Mr. Charles Delafoſſe, maſter of the
Boarding-fchool, Richmond-green
Mr. Jofeph Davis, Parifh-Clerk of
Peterfham
* Mr. Lockyer Davis, Bookfeller, two
copies
Mr. Raymond Davis .
Mr. Edward Davidfon

E.

* The Right Hon. the Countefs Dow-
ager of Effingham
* The Hon. and Right Rev. the Lord
Bifhop of Exeter
Mr. Dilman Englehart
Mr. Edmead
Mr. Edwards, Surgeon

F.

* The Right Hon. Lady Charlotte
Finch
The Right Hon. Lady Fitzwilliam
Lieutenant General Fitzwilliam

The

The Rev. Thomas Francklin, D. D.
Vicar of Ware, Herts, and Chaplain
in Ordinary to his Majesty

The Rev. Claudius Fonnereau, L.L. D.

* Thomas Edwards Freeman, Esq;

* Peter Floyer, Esq;

Edward Fletcher, Esq;

The Rev. Mr. Fayting, Rector of St.
Martin's Outwich, London

Mr. William Faden, five copies

Mr. Farmer

Mr. Fawson

G.

* The Right Hon. the Countess of
Greenwich

* Baron Grothous

* The Rev. —— Gooch, D. D. Pre-
bendary of Ely

Lady Grant

Mrs. Graves

Mrs. Gualtier

* Mrs. Gardiner, of Twickenham

Mrs. Gaudy, Governess of the Boarding-school at Richmond

Mrs. Green, Governess of the Boarding-school at Hadleigh

Miss Gooch

Miss Guy

Miss S. Guy

* William Gardiner, Esq;

John Gray, Esq;

John Henry Grose, Esq;

—— Goodchild, Esq;

Edward Gascoigne, Esq;

* Joshua Glover, Esq;

* Mrs Glover

* Charles Grignion, Esq; Engraver

Augustine Greenland, Esq; Secretary
in the Chancery-court

Mordecai Green, Esq;

* John Guise, Esq;

* Mrs. Guise

Mr. Job Gardiner

Mr. James Guillet

H.

* The Right Hon. the Earl of Harrington

* The Right Hon. Lady Harrington

* The Right Hon. the Earl of Hard-
wicke

The Right Hon. Lady Howe

The Hon. H. Hobart

The Hon. Mrs. Hobart

George Harris, L.L. D.

John Hawkesworth, L.L. D.

* Mrs. Houblon

Mrs. Hunter

Mrs. Holman

Mrs. Anne Handley

Mrs. Sarah Handley

Mrs. Hardinge

Mrs. Huddon

Mrs. Herbert

Mrs. Holroyd

Mrs. Harriot Hales

Miss Howard

* Miss Hardinge

* Miss Juliana Hardinge

Miss Emma Maria Hillier

Miss Charlotte Hillier

John Holroyd, Esq;

Pennell Hawkins, Esq; Surgeon to the
Royal Household

Capt. John Hamilton, of Montpelier-
row

—— Heron, Esq;

* Isaac Henckell, Esq;

Tilman Henckell, Esq;

Miles Halley, Esq;

Percivall Hart, Esq;

—— Holman, Esq;

George Hardinge, Esq;

* Leonard Hammond, Esq; two Books

* John Haverfield, Esq;

John Haverfield, Esq; Jun.

Thomas Haverfield, Esq;

Mr. William Haverfield, of University-
College, Oxford

The

SUBSCRIBERS NAMES.

The Rev. Mr. Samuel Hemming, Chaplain to the Right Reverend the Lord Bishop of London
Mr. James Howard
Mr. William Henley
Mr. Horsfield, Bookseller, two Copies
Mr. Joseph Hall, Bookseller
Mr. Thomas Hill
Mr. Joseph Hillier
Mr. Hyde, of Cambridge
Mr. Hall, Bookbinder, Beaufort Buildings

I.

The Rev. James Ibbetson, D. D. Rector of Bushey, Herts, and Archdeacon of St. Alban's
Robert Wallace Johnson, M. D.
The Rev. Mr. Jeffreys, of Isleworth
Mrs James
Miss Irish
Mr. Jackson, Surgeon
Mr. Ibbetson

K.

The Rev. Thomas Knowles, D. D. Rector of Ickworth, Preacher of St. Mary's, Bury St. Edmunds
Mrs. Knapp
Mrs. Kranen
Mrs. Elizabeth Knapton
* Mrs. King
Thomas King, Esq;
J. Knapton, Esq;
Ralph Knox, Esq;
Richard Knowler, Esq;
* Joshua Kirby, Esq; Designer in Perspective to their Majesties, and F. R. S.
William Kirby, Esq; of the Board of Works
Mr. King, of the Ferry
Mr. Kingsbury

L.
Mrs. Loydd

Mrs. Levi
Mrs. Langford
Caleb Lomax, Esq; of Childwick, Bury
Henry Leaves, Esq;
Charles Leigh, Esq;
The Rev. Mr. Larkum
The Rev. Mr. Langford, of Eton
Mr. Langford, Surgeon
Mr. Philip Laggatt
Mr. George Long

M.

* His Grace the Duke of Montague
His Excellency M. Moussin Pouffin, Minister from Russia
The Rev. Bernard Mills, D. D. Rector of Hitcham
The Rev. Mr. John Morgan, Chancellor of St. David's
Mrs. Marks
Mrs. Middleton
Mrs. Marten
Mrs. Jane Moore
Charles Morris, Esq;
Thomas Morson, Esq;
Samuel Moody, Esq;
Andrew Millar, Esq;
James Miller, Esq;
Thomas Melmouth, Esq;
* —— Messman, Esq;
Jeremiah Meyer, Esq;
Thomas Metholde, Esq;
Mr. Merrill, Bookseller, two Copies
Mr. Benjamin Martin
* Mr. Morris

N.

The Rev. —— Neden, D. D.
* Dr. Nares, of the Royal Chapel
Ditto, four Copies
Mrs Newton
* Miss Noy
* James Norman, Esq;
The Rev. Mr. Nott

* The

SUBSCRIBERS NAMES.

* The Rev. Mr. Naylor, Master of the Boarding-school, Acton-green
Mr. Norton

O.
* The Right Hon. George Onflow
Thomas Overton, Esq;
Mrs. Orton
Mr. Orton
Mr. Owen, Bookseller, two Copies

P.
The Right Hon. the Lady Juliana Penn
* Sir Samuel Prime
* Lady Prime
Sir James Porter
General Paterson
* Samuel Pechell, Esq; Master in Chancery, two Copies
Lieutenant-Colonel Paul Pechell
Mrs. Paten
Mrs. Palmer
Mrs. Pritchard
Miss Priaulx
William Patoun, Esq;
Lewis Perrin, Esq;
Charles Pearce, Esq;
Stephen Pitt, Esq;
Hinchley Phipps, Esq;
—— Palmer, Esq;
John Price, Esq;
James Payne, Esq; of the Board of Works
The Rev. Mr. Pridie, Rector of St. Alban's Abbey
Mr. Thomas Payne, Bookseller, two Copies
Mr. Giles Panchen, of Doctors Commons
Mr. Edward Prockter, Junior
Mr. Palmer
Mr. Price, Timber-merchant
Mr. James Perrigall

Q.
Her Grace the Dutchess of Queensberry

R
Sir William Richardson
Major Roberts, of Portsmouth
* Miss Roberts
Captain Rowley, of the Navy
Mrs. Russell
Mrs. Russell, of Ormond row
Mrs. Martha Roberts
Mrs. Russel, of George-street
* Mrs. Reessin, of Shene
* Miss Margaret Robertson
* Miss Isabella Robertson
* Miss Anne Robinson, of Kew
* Miss Mary Fanny Robinson
Miss Sarah Rhoades
James Ross, Esq;
William Roberts, Esq;
George Robertson, Esq; of the Navy
William Robertson, Esq; East-India service
Charles Le Roche, Esq;
Thomas Robinson, Esq; Page to the Princes
* Mr. William Robertson, Surgeon
Mr. Runnington
Mr. Thomas Reading, of Hedgerley
Mr. Charles Reading
Mr. Roberts, of Brentford
Mr. Jonathan Robotham
Mr. Matthew Randall, Junior

S.
Sir Charles Sheffield, Bart.
Lady Seabright
Baron de Stark
The Rev. H. Matthew Schutz, Rector of March Gibbons, and Chaplain in Ordinary to his Majesty
Miss Schwellenberg
Mrs. Skinner
Mrs. Siddall
Mrs Stubbs
* Mrs. Selwyn
* Miss Frances Smith, of Orange-street
Mrs.

SUBSCRIBERS NAMES.

Mrs. Starkie

Mrs. Spilfbury, Governefs of the Boarding-fchool at Hammerfmith

Samuel Smith, Efq; of Briftol

Dutton Seaman, Efq; Inner Temple

—— Symondfon, Efq; Secretary to his
Grace the Archbifhop of Canterbury

* Matthew Skinner, Efq;

Daniel Le Sueur, Efq;

William Smith, Efq; Auditor of the
War-office

James Sayer, Efq; Deputy-fteward of
Richmond Manor

John Salter, Efq;

Thomas Smith, Efq;

* John Somner Sedley, Efq;

The Rev. Mr. Soame, of Milden-hall

Mr. Shenton

Mr. William Strudwick, Surgeon

* Mr. Thomas Smith, of Orange-ftreet

Mr. Clement Smith

Mr. Richard Smith

Mr. Stallard

Mr. Francis Stone

Mr. Edward Smith

Mr. Richard Seaman

* Mr. Smith, Mafter of the Boarding-
fchool at Richmond

Mr. Charles Scott

T.

Sir Edmund Thomas, Bart.

* Mrs. Tunftall

* Henry St. John Darell Trelawny,
Efq;

Witchcot Turner, Efq;

William Turner, Efq;

John Thompfon, Efq;

* Peter Theobald, Efq;

Thomas Tunftall. Efq;

John Thomas, Efq;

—— Turton, Efq;

The Rev. Mr. George Tilfon

Mr. James Trimmer, Junior

Mr. William Telphord

V.

Sir Francis Vincent, Bart.

W.

The Right Hon. the Earl of
Winchelfea

* The Right Rev. the Lord Bifhop of
Winchefter

Sir Booth Williams, Bart.

Mrs. Wray

Mrs Sarah Wadefon

Mrs. Wilkes

Mrs. Wright, of Newport-ftreet

* Mifs Anna Maria Wotton

Mifs J. M. Wiltfchut

* Mrs. Wood, Governefs of the Boarding-fchool at St. Edmund's-bury

Mifs Hannah M. M. Wood

James Witchurch, Efq;

Thomas Howlett Warren, Efq;

** Jofeph Wilton, Efq; of the Royal
Academy, Statuary to his Majefty,
two Copies

—— Watts, Efq; Deputy Treafurer
to the Princefs of Wales

* George Wilfon, Efq; of Symond's-
Inn

John Wollafton, Efq;

Lewis Way, Efq;

Benjamin Way, Efq;

William White, Efq;

George Wood, Efq;

Daniel Wray, Efq;

Daniel Wife, Efq;

Groves Wheeler, Efq;

* George Wegg, Efq;

William Wright, Efq; three Copies

* Samuel Wale, Efq; of the Royal
Academy

The Rev. Mr. George Wollafton,
F R. S. Rector of Stratford, St.
Mary, Suffolk

The Rev. Mr. Frederick Wollafton,
Preacher at St. James's, Bury St.
Edmonds

The

SUBSCRIBERS NAMES.

The Rev. Mr. Woodcock, Vicar of
    Watford
* The Rev. Mr. George Wakefield,
    Vicar of Kingston upon Thames
Mr. Wilson, of the W. H. College
* Mr. Watts, of Thames-street
Mr. Webster
Mr. Waterman
Mr. Richard Walklin, Schoolmaster at
    Richmond

Mr. John Wood, of Ipswich
Mr. Thomas Woodgate, Bookseller at
    Brighthelmstone
Mr. Samuel Witchingham, Junior
Mr. Ward
Mr. George Warren
            Y.
Shute Shrimpton Yeamans, Esq;
Mrs. Yeames, Governess of the Board-
    ing-school, in Ormond-row

⁎ The impression of this Work consists only of Five Hundred Copies,
viz. — One Hundred on *Writing Paper*, for those Names marked with
Asterisks. — Four Hundred on *common Paper*. — The Purchasers are as-
sured that,—in whatever shape the ETHIC AMUSEMENTS may hereafter appear,—the Version of BOETIUS shall never, by the Editor's permission, be
re-printed; whereby that excellent Piece of moral Philosophy will impart a
value to the Subscribers Books, not only from its real merit, but from its
scarceness.

July 1770.

☞ Omissions or Mistakes in the foregoing List of Names may be rectified,
if pointed out to the Editor before *Christmas* next; at which Time the
Subscription will be finally closed, and should any Copies then remain un-
sold, the Price will be raised to *Two Guineas* the Writing-paper, and *One
Guinea and a Half* the common Paper.

THE

PROPHECY:

An ODE.

QUA NIHIL MAJUS, MELIUSVE TERRIS
FATA DONAVERE, BONIQUE DIVI
NEC DABUNT, QUAMVIS REDEANT IN AURUM
        TEMPORA PRISCUM.   HORAT.

Than whom the Gods ne'er gave, or bounteous fate
To human kind a gift more good or great,
Nor from their treasures shall again unfold,
Though Time roll backward to his ancient gold.

                              FRANCIS.

O D E

T O

H E R   M A J E S T Y;

W I T H   A   C O P Y   O F   T H E

E T H I C   A M U S E M E N T S.

M O S T   H U M B L Y   P R E S E N T E D

B Y   T H E   E D I T O R.

I.

TREMBLING I wake the lyre; for, ah! what ftrain
    What energy of facred fong
May fpeak HER merit?—nor profane
 Bleft CAROLETTA's name, fo long
The joy of ev'ry heart, and theme of ev'ry tongue?

                        Come

II.

Come GRATITUDE! thou _SERAPH_ rob'd in fire,
  Sole Sovran of my paffive mind,
Be thou my Mufe; and, oh, infpire
  Thy raptur'd votary to find
Fit Eulogy for Her — THE FRIEND OF HUMAN KIND!

III.

As PARENT, — could'ft thou paint her holy care,
  Watching with all the _Charities_;
As WIFE — a pattern for the Fair:
  What boots the blazon with the wife?
Who read Her commendation in a Monarch's eyes.

IV.

Her _Bounty_, like the golden font of day,
  Could'ft thou defcribe in numbers free,
Effufing wide its genial ray,
  From greatnefs even down to —— me;
Say, — what avails to prove what all confefs, and fee?

V.

CÆCILIA now, SHE wakes the foul of fong,
  And gives the lyre to ecftafy;
Now fhines PENELOPE among
  HER chofen female band, who ply
The needle's art, and fix the flow'rs perennial dye.

The

AN ODE.

VI.

The daughters of ingenuous Poverty,
   (Such glories in HER annals shine)
Hence eat the bread of Industry;
   Their manners with their art refine,
And emulate their QUEEN—A CHRISTIAN HEROINE!

VII.

Hence, ye Prophane!—Let no unhallow'd sight
   Intrude upon her secret hour;
Her blue eye lifts its humid light
   In frequent homage to that pow'r,
Who makes her Portion GEORGE, and Paradise her Dow'r.

VIII.

'Twas in the Reign of GEORGE THE GOOD,"—so *Fame*
   To future ages shall report —
" *Virtue* with CAROLETTA came,
   " And fix'd her residence at Court,
" Then *Greatness* learn'd to lean on *Goodness* for support.

IX.

" Bless'd be that memorable Holiday
   " Which brought—see BRITAIN's Genius smile —
" The *living treasure* o'er the sea,
   " T'enrich and dignify this Isle !
" *Sincerely Christian*, then was Woman's highest style.

                 * 2   " Hence

X.

" Hence the true Eafe of nuptial happinefs,
  " Her fair example could reftore ;
" And hence fhall future GEORGES blefs
    " The world: and ALBION's fartheft fhore
" Sound CAROLETTA's name, till time fhall be no more.

XI.

Go Mufe ! nor at the Throne acceptance fear,
  Religion's Heav'n-directed look
Makes all *Amufement Ethic* there :
  Ev'n Majefty thy fong fhall brook,
" And from its meaning well, fee merit in the Book.

KEW, *May* 10, 1768.

O D E

T O

HER ROYAL HIGHNESS

THE PRINCESS DOWAGER OF WALES;

WITH A COPY OF THE

ETHIC AMUSEMENTS.

MOST HUMBLY PRESENTED

BY THE EDITOR.

I.

MOTHER of GEORGE !—an awful name,
 Which late pofterity fhall blefs,
When grateful BRITAIN fhall enquire of Fame,
 The fource of all her happinefs ;
And thro' a long illuftrious Race,
Backward to thee the various Virtues trace.

II.

Ah, deign, all-gracious ! to receive,
 (Refpect can render trifles dear)
Nor more the rich, nor more the great can give —
 An offering from a heart fincere :
To Heav'n, alike accepted, come
The fingle heifer, and the hecatomb.

Infolvent

AN ODE.

III.

Insolvent e'en in thanks till now,
  The Muse would vindicate her right
To pay — 'tis all her feeble pow'rs allow,
  One humble, tributary mite:
May that her *fealty* record !
And *thy* acceptance bland becomes her best reward.

IV.

If aught of moral good, or fair ;
  If aught that dignifies man's breast,
Aright her imitative page declare ;
  And all AUGUSTA stands confest :
To HER those happier lines of right belong,
For who inspires the Bard, perforce must take the Song.

V.

And thou, old THAMES ! whose sacred stream,
  Calm, clear, majestically deep,
Resembles best my heart enobling theme,
  Say, as I trod thy flow'ry steep,
Did e'er ambition on my soul intrude,
Save to evince my FAITH, and glowing GRATITUDE ?

VI.

Enough for me, in some retreat,
  Unheeded by the public eye,
To steal thro' life with noiseless pace, and eat
  My bread with peace and privacy ;
Appease each hope, and fears tumultuous strife,
And read my duty in my SOVRAN's Life.

KEW, *July* 4, 1768.

S O N N E T

T O

H I S R O Y A L H I G H N E S S

T H E PRINCE OF WALES;

W I T H A M.S. V E R S I O N O F

F E N E L O N'S F A B L E S.

M O S T H U M B L Y P R E S E N T E D

B Y T H E E D I T O R.

I.

GEORGE, Prince of Wales! Great Britain's dearest hope,
   Round whom the winged sanctities of Heaven,
Ere wakes the *Bridegroom Sun*, to when aslope
   He beams his western glory; night and even,
Spread their sure panoply: — What shall a Bard
Of earth present, worthy that minds regard —
A CHARLOTTE's Pupil, and an Angel's Ward?

> Line 3. *Bridegroom Sun*, alluding to Psalm xix. 5.
> —— 7. *Angel's Ward*, alluding to St. Matthew xviii. 10.

And

II.

And yet — fond wifh ! ev'n this *poor Book* may prove,
   Should'ft thou its merit by its meaning weigh,
How burns my bofom with refpectful love,
   And pants the debt of Gratitude to pay :
Admitted to that * SHRINE thy MOTHER gave —
—High place can Books, as well as Authors fave —
One work of ours perchance, may triumph o'er the grave.

* An elegant Book-cafe prefented by her Majefty, to his Royal Highnefs on his Birth-day 1768.

KEW, *Auguft* 12, 1769.

ETHIC

TALES AND FABLES.

INVENTED

FOR THE EDUCATION OF A PRINCE.

BY

FRANCOIS DE SALIGNAC DE LA MOTTE
FENELON,

ARCHBISHOP, AND DUKE OF CAMBRAY.

FROM THE FRENCH.

By D. BELLAMY.

FICTION IS OF THE ESSENCE OF POETRY, AS WELL AS PAINTING: THERE IS A
RESEMBLANCE IN ONE OF HUMAN BODIES, THINGS, AND ACTIONS, WHICH
ARE NOT REAL, AND IN THE OTHER OF A TRUE STORY BY A FICTION.

DRYDEN.

FENELON's

TALES and FABLES.

FABLE ·I.

The ADVENTURES of ARISTONÖUS.

SOPHRONYMUS, having met with a long feries of difappoint-ments both at home and abroad, and being thereby reduced to the lowest ebb of fortune, fought confolation from his virtue in the Ifle of *Delos*. There he tuned his golden lyre; there fang the wonders of the *Delian* God. He made his court there to the Mufes, who proved as kind as they were fair. The wond'rous works of nature were the conftant objects of his contem-plation: there he ftudied the revolutions of the Heavens, and all the ftarry train, the beauteous order of the elements, the fabrick of the terreftrial globe, which he was ever meafuring with his compafs, the various qualities of plants, and ftructure of the bru-tal world;—but above all, in this retreat he pried with a more cu-rious eye into himfelf; with pleafure reflected on his fuperior facul-ties, and practifed all the virtues that adorn the foul. Thus dif-

B

trefs

treſs did not debaſe his noble mind; it only changed the ſcene, and gave him new glory by the alteration.

Whilſt thus he lived poor, but content in his retirement! he ſpied a venerable, grave old man, juſt landed on the Iſland. This ſtranger with ſurprize ſurveyed the ſea-banks, well-knowing that the Iſle once floated here and there: but fixed his eyes with more attention on that ſide, where the ſmall hills, forever verdant, reared up their heads above the rocks. He thought he never could admire enough the chryſtal ſprings, and rapid floods, that water this delightful country. Slowly he moved along towards the hallowed groves, which ſhade all round the temple of the God. He gazed with pleaſure on thoſe ever-greens, which the bleak north-winds durſt not blaſt. With curious eyes he viewed the beauties of the temple; its *Parian* marble, white as the new-fallen ſnow; its ſtately pillars of ſolid jaſper. SOPHRONYMUS, with equal curioſity, obſerved the good old man. His ſilver beard fell graceful on his breaſt. His face, tho' wrinkled, no ways was deformed. As yet, he knew none of the cares of age. His eyes were quick and lively; his ſtature tall and majeſtic; his years, however, made him decline a little; and when he walked, he wore an ivory ſtaff. SOPHRONYMUS approached, and thus addreſſed him: What is it, venerable ſir, you ſeek for here? You ſeem a perfect ſtranger to the place. If it is the temple of the God; yonder it ſtands, and, if you pleaſe, I will conduct you thither. I reverence the Gods, and know my duty to a ſtranger.

The old Gentleman replied;—with pleaſure I accept your friendly offer. May the kind Gods reward your love to ſtrangers! Lead to the temple.—As they walked along, he told SOPHRONYMUS his adventures. My name, ſaid he, is ARISTONÖUS: I was born at *Clazomene*, a town in *Ionia*, ſituate in that pleaſant coaſt that advances towards the ſea, and ſeems as if it joined the Iſle of *Chios*,

the

the native country of immortal *Homer*. My parents, tho' poor, were both of an illuſtrious family. POLISTRATUS, that was my father's name, being encumbered with too large a family, unkindly ordered a friend of his at *Teos* to expoſe me naked to the world, a tender, helpleſs infant. A charitable old woman of *Erythrea*, who lived hard by, commiſerated my unhappy ſtate, and reared me with goat's milk as her own. But as her circumſtances were very narrow, when I was capable of ſervice, ſhe ſold me to a merchant who conveyed me, as his ſlave, to *Lycia*. He ſold me again at *Patara* —luckily for me—to *Alcinus*, a Gentleman of fortune and diſtin-guiſhed merit. This *Alcinus* was a ſecond father to me in my youth. I was ſo happy as to be thought good-natured, ſober, ho-neſt, well-inclined, and attentive to all good advice. By his direc-tion I applied myſelf to *Apollo*'s favourite arts. Muſic and ex-erciſe were my amuſements; but his healing faculty my chief re-gard. I ſoon made large improvements in that ſo neceſſary ſcience ; and aſſiſted by the inſpiration of the God, found out a thouſand curious ſecrets. *Alcinus*, who ſtill grew more indulgent as I ad-vanced in years, well-pleaſed with the ſucceſs of all his cares, made me a freeman, and ſent me to *Damocles*, the King of *Lycaonia*; a Prince much given to luxury and eaſe, who made this life his care, and trembled at the thoughts of death. The monarch, to attach me to his intereſt, made me rich and great. *Damocles*, ſome few years after died. His ſon, incenſed againſt me, by the inſtigation of ſome paraſites about him, gave me a diſtaſte to the pomp and grandeur of a court. In ſhort, I had a ſtrong incli-nation to reviſit *Lycia*, where I had ſpent my younger years with ſo much ſatisfaction. I lived in hopes of ſeeing once again my patron, my foſter-father, my benefactor. On my firſt arrival I heard the melancholy news that he was dead ; that juſt before his deceaſe he loſt his whole eſtate, and ſuffered manfully the frowns of fortune,

and the cares of age. I vifited his tomb, ftrewed flowers upon
his venerable afhes, and bathed them with my tears. To perpetu-
ate his memory, I ordered his character to be engraved upon the
ftone; and then enquired into his family-concerns. I was informed
that *Orchilochus* was his only furviving fon, who difdaining to live
in penury, and in a cottage, where his father had before him lived
in fuch grandeur and repute, was refolved to lead a folitary life in
fome far diftant Ifland. *Orchilochus*, it feems, foon after was caft
away upon the coaft of *Carphatus*; fo that the whole race of my
dear friend and benefactor then was quite extinct. I determined
immediately to purchafe the eftate, where formerly he lived in eafe
and plenty. With pleafure I furveyed the fruitful fields around,
which brought to my remembrance pleafures paft, and the dear
image of my worthy mafter. I could fcarce perfuade myfelf but
that I was young again, and gay, as when I ferved *Alcinus*. Soon
as I had fettled this purchafe with his creditors, affairs, of a quite
different nature, called me again to *Clazomene*. My father *Peliftra-
tus*, and *Phidilis* my mother, were both dead. My reftlefs, uneafy
brothers, were forever at variance one with another. No fooner was
I arrived at *Clazomene*, but I made myfelf known to them, in the
tattered garb of a poor, miferable flave, overwhelmed with his
misfortunes, and fhewed the marks that infants generally bear,
who are expofed as I was. They were nettled at this new difcovery,
nor wanted unexpected heirs to make their little lefs. They ftre-
nuoufly infifted, I was a bold impoftor, and denied my right in
open court. In return to this ungenerous, unnatural declaration, I
publicly refigned my title, confented to be deemed a perfect ftranger,
and moved that they might equally difclaim their right in me. A
decree was paft accordingly; then I threw off the flave; difcovered
the treafure I had on board; affured them, that I was the fame
                                                                ARIS-

ARISTODÖUS, who had long been the peculiar favourite of *Damocles*, the late King of *Lycaonia*, and that I never had been married.

My brothers foon repented of their coldnefs towards me, and hoping ftill in time to be my heirs, were obfequious to the laft degree, and ftudied, but to no purpofe, to oblige me. Their perpetual jars compelled them to expofe that little they had left to public fale. I was the faireft purchafer; and they, with fhame and deep reluctance, faw him legally poffeffed of all their father had, whofe right to the leaft part, they had fo publicly contefted. In a fhort time, by their ill conduct, all grew miferably poor. But after I had humbled them, and made them feel my juft refentment, I gave them large demonftrations of love and friendfhip. Freely I forgave them all; received them in my houfe; by proper prefents, put it in their powers to trade abroad, and get eftates. The family was all harmony; they and their children lived with me in perfect peace. They all efteemed me as their common parent. By this happy union, and their diligence and application, all became confiderably rich. In the mean time, you fee, old age knocks loudly at my door, covers my head with fnow, furrows my face, and warns me that my healthful days are not of long duration Once more, therefore, I determined, before this feeble lamp of life was quite extinguifhed, to revifit that favourite fpot of ground, more dear to me than even my native country, that *Lycia*, where I ftudied to be wife and virtuous, under the kind guidance of my good old mafter. In my paffage thither, I was credibly informed by a merchant of the *Cyclad Iflands*, that one of *Orchilochus*'s fons ftill lived at *Delos*; and practifed all the virtues of his god-like grandfire. Whereupon I immediately declined my intended voyage; and under the protection of the *Delian* God, arrived in fafety on this happy Ifland, in hopes to find the dear remains of one, to whom I owe my life, my liberty, my all: My days are almoft now fpun out to their full

length:

length : the cruel *Parcæ*, foes to that downy reft which *Jove* be-
ftows fo feldom upon mortals, will quickly cut the feeble thread !
O ! could thefe eyes but once behold the grandfon of my dear, dear
mafter, freely I'd prefs into Death's icy arms ! Speak then, O fpeak,
my hofpitable friend, have you ever heard of fuch a virtuous youth ?
Can you direct me where to find him ? If you can, may the kind
Gods reward you for the favour ! May they prolong your happy life,
'till your childrens' children dance upon your knees, and afk
your bleffing ! May peace and plenty, the beft fruits of virtue, ever
attend your numerous progeny ! At the clofe of this kind prayer of
ARISTONÖUS, tears, fhed from joy and grief, like kindly fhowers,
flowed down SOPHRONYMUS's checks.   His tranfport ftopped the
organs of his fpeech ; filent, he threw his arms around the old
man's neck, embraced, and preffed him clofe : but at the laft, words
intermingled with fighs found out their way.—O ! venerable Sir,
I am the youth you look for ;—I am the grandfon of your friend
Alcinus: and from the recital of your wond'rous ftory, am perfuaded, fully perfuaded, that Heaven has fent you here to mitigate my forrows.   Gratitude, which long fince—like *Aftræa*—had
forfook the world, is now returned in you.   I had heard, indeed,
when but a child, that a gentleman of fortune and diftinguifhed
merit, who lived in *Lycaonia*, had been educated by my grand-fa-
ther : but as my father *Orchilochus* died young, when I was a poor,
helplefs infant, you may imagine my ideas of thofe things were but
confufed.   I was loth, on fuch weak motives, to go to *Lycaonia* ;
I chofe rather to continue here in quiet, alleviating my forrows
by a philofophical contempt of grandeur and magnificence, and an
agreeable cultivation of the mufes in the temple of *Apollo.*   Mi-
nerva, who inftructs mankind, that nature is fufficed with but a
little, and that true happinefs confifts in a contented mind, has
hitherto fupported me, and amply made amends for all my loffes.

SOPHRO-

SOPHRONYMUS, soon as he had spoke thefe words, finding himfelf before the temple-gate, propofed to ARISTONÖUS to enter in,
and offer up their mutual prayers and praifes to the *Delian* God.
The propofal was approved; with awful reverence two lambs,
white as the new-fallen fnow, and a young heifer, with a crefcent
on his forehead, juft between his horns, were laid upon the altar.
There they hailed the God of Day; there in melodious numbers
praifed the fun, who, in his radiant orb, illumines heaven and
earth; who rolls around the year, makes all the arts and fciences
his care, and animates the facred nine. Their homage to the God
thus paid, they fpent the remnant of the day, alternately recounting
their adventures. SOPHRONYMUS conducted to his houfe the good
old man, and entertained him with the fame refpect as he would
have fhewn *Alcinus*, had he then been living. The day following
both agreed to fail for *Lycia*. ARISTONÖUS led his companion into
a fertile country, on the verdant borders of the river *Xanthus*, in
whofe tranfparent ftreams *Apollo*, wearied with the chace, and covered
with duft, fo frequently had plunged, and wafhed his golden locks.
Willows and poplars ftood in rows along the river fide, within
whofe tender verdant boughs a thoufand pretty birds concealed their
nefts, and warbled night and day. The river, falling from the fummit of a rock, dafhed down her noify, foaming billows into a little
channel paved with pebbles. A golden harveft covered all the plain.
Fruit-trees and vines rofe, like an amphitheatre, all round the little
hills. There lavifh nature had adorned the year; clear was the
fky, ferene the air, and the earth ready to produce her ftores, with
gratitude to crown the labours of the fwain. As they advanced
ftill higher up the river, SOPHRONYMUS perceived a little country
feat, not gay, but regularly built. No marble pillars, no coftly
figures, wrought in filver, gold, or ivory, adorned the out-fide; no
purple furniture was feen within. Every thing, however, was neat,
clean,

clean, and convenient, tho' no ways oftentatious. In the middle
of the court, a little fountain played its waters high, which, as they
fell, formed a delightful rill, whose verdant banks were all enamelled with the gayeft flowers. The gardens were but fmall, yet
plentifully ftored with various fruits and falutary plants. On each
fide of the garden was a pleafant grove, whose lofty trees feemed
coetaneous with their mother earth : whose branches were fo
thick, fo interwoven, that no fun-beams e'er could pierce them.
They withdrew into a fpacious parlour, and there refreshed themfelves with fuch repaft, as nature from the gardens had provided ;
wherein no coftly foreign fruits were introduced, fo often purchafed,
and fo much admired in cities. They had milk in plenty ; fweeter
than that *Apollo's* cattle yielded, when fhepherd to *Admetus*. ' They
had honey more delicious than the product of the *Sicilian* Bees in
Hybla, or thofe of *Attica* on mount *Hymettus*. They had ftore of
beans and peafe, and various fruits before them but that moment
gathered. Their wine, which was racked off from ftately jars into
fmall, well-wrought bowls, was of a finer flavour, and more racy
than the nectar of the Gods. ARISTONÖUS, during this frugal,
but delightful entertainment, would not fit down at table. At firft,
he made a thoufand little excufes to conceal his modefty ; but when
at laft SOPHRONYMUS was too importunate, he owned the caufe :
declared he could not make himfelf fo free, and fo familiar with
the grandfon of *Alcinus*, behind whofe chair he had fo many years
attended in that very parlour. Here, Sir, faid he, my good old
mafter always dined ; there he converfed with his familiar friends ;
there followed all his innocent diverfions. *Hefiod* and *Homer* were
his old companions here ; and there, Sir, was his favourite bed-
room. In friendly recollection of thefe various circumftances his
tender heart began to melt, and tears ran trickling down his cheeks.
After their repaft was over, he conducted SOPHRONYMUS into the
adjacent

adjacent meadows, to take a view of his large cattle, which ranged at will and lowed along the river. Then they furveyed his numerous flocks, as they returned from their fat paſtures. The little wanton lambs played near the bleating ewes, whoſe udders fwelled with milk. They found no ſervants idle ; all were induſtrious in their ſeveral vocations : work ſeemed a pleaſure for ſo good a maſter ; one whom they loved ſo well ; and one, who ſweetened all their labours.

ARISTONÖUS having now ſhewn SOPHRONYMUS his houſe, his flaves, his herds, his flocks, and fertile meadows, thus addreſſed him : With tranſport I behold you now poſſeſſed of what your anceſtors enjoyed before you. Happy am I ! thus to have power to reinſtate you on that very ſpot, where I ſo long had ſerved the good *Alcinus.* Enjoy in peace that which long ſince was his. Make yourſelf happy, but be cautious ; and by your prudent conduct, may your decline of life be replete with better fortune than marked your venerable father's latter days. — Immediately he made the eſtate over to SOPHRONYMUS by a legal conveyance ; and declared he would diſinherit ſuch of his relations, as ſhould ungratefully preſume to diſpute his title. ARISTONÖUS had ſtill further favours to beſtow. Before this deed of gift was executed, he furniſhed the houſe anew; made it at all points decent and compleat ; without things gaudy and ſuperfluous. The barns he ſtored with the rich treaſures of the Goddeſs *Ceres* ; the cellars with the choiceſt wines of *Chios,* neat and racy, fit to be ſerved up at *Jove*'s table by *Ganymede* or *Hebe.* — To theſe he added choice *Parmenian* wines, the honey of *Hymettus* and of *Hybla,* in large quantities ; and *Attic* oils almoſt as ſweet, and of as fine a flavour. Moreover, he heaped up a boundleſs ſtock of the fineſt wool, white as unſullied ſnow, the treaſures formerly of tender ſheep that fed en the *Arcadian* mountains and *Sicilian* plains. With theſe valuable additions was the houſe made over to SOPHRONYMUS. He cloſed his bounty with a

C   ſpecific

F E N E L O N's

ſpecific legacy of fifty *Euboic* talents, reſerving to his own relations his ſeveral eſtates in *Clazomene*, *Smyrna*, *Lebedos*, and *Colophon*; all of conſiderable value. ARISTONÖUS having thus ſettled his affairs to his entire ſatisfaction, reimbarked on board his veſſel, bound for *Ionia*. SOPHRONYMUS overwhelmed with ſuch a flood of favors, waited on him to the ſhip; and as the tears ran trickling down his cheeks, with filial tenderneſs careſſed him, and called him as they went along, his father. The winds proved favourable, and ARISTONÖUS ſoon arrived ſafe at home. None of his relations ever preſumed to murmur at his bounty to SOPHRONYMUS. My friends, ſaid he, I have now made my will ; and thereby have declared, that all my effects, real and perſonal, without reſtriction, ſhall be ſold, and given to the poor *Ionians* ; in caſe any one of you hereafter ſhall diſpute my free donation to the grandſon of *Alcinus*. The good old man long lived in peace ; long he enjoyed the good things of this life, which the kind Gods beſtowed as the rewards of virtue. His age did not prevent him, once a year, from viſiting SOPHRONYMUS at *Lycia*, and ſacrificing on the tomb of good *Alcinus*, which he had decorated with new erections, and moſt curious carved work.—He by his will directed, that his body, after his deceaſe, ſhould be interred in the ſame tomb, that even in death he might embrace his maſter. SOPHRONYMUS, as each revolving ſpring came on, impatient to behold his friend, forever fixt his eyes upon the ſhore, in hopes to ſpy the bark, which at that ſeaſon brought his dear ARISTONÖUS to his arms. Each year he had the pleaſure to deſcry from far the wiſh'd-for veſſel, ploughing the briny waves, and moving towards him. The diſtant proſpect pleaſed him infinitely more than all the beauties which the ſpring can boaſt of, when the winter's rage abates:

This ſo much long'd-for ſhip one ſpring ne'er came at all. SOPHRONYMUS ſighed from his inward ſoul. His ſecret anguiſh and diſtracting fears were legible upon his face.—Soft, downy ſleep ne'er ne'er clofed his weary eye-lids. He had no relifh for the moft coftly dainties. Reftlefs he fpent the tedious hours; each little noife alarmed him : his eyes were ever wand'ring towards the port, and he would every moment afk after the *Ionian* veffels.—One comes at laft:—but oh !—no ARISTONÖUS was there.—Only his venerable afhes in a filver urn. *Amphicles,* an old gentleman, and bofom-friend of the deceafed, his faithful executor, was the fole melancholy bearer.—When he firft approached, SOPHRONYMUS had no words to tell his grief:—Both mingled fighs in a dumb fcene of forrow. SOPHRONYMUS firft kiffed the urn, then bathed it with his tears;—words—at laft found out their way.—O thou venerable, good old man !—All the pleafures I e'er enjoyed flowed from thy bounty : now all my joy, my comfort, all that is left in life fleets after thee. Thefe eyes fhall never fee thee more; death now would be thrice welcome, could I but fly to thee, attend thee in the *Elyfian* fields, where thy bleft fhade enjoys eternal reft : and fuch pleafures as the Gods referve for virtuous men: Thou haft brought back again, in thefe degenerate times, religion, juftice and gratitude on earth. In thefe iron days, thou haft difplayed the innocence and beauties of the golden age. The Gods, before they crowned thee with the glories of the juft, granted thee length of happy days. But, alas! he, who deferves to be immortal, often dies the fooneft. Thy verdant fields, thy flow'ry gardens, now have no charms for me; now thou art abfent, every place feems defert. O bleft fhade ! when fhall I follow thee ? ye dear remains ! had you fenfation, you would furely feel new pleafure in mingling with the afhes of *Alcinus.* Mine fhall one day be mingled too with yours. Till that day comes, I fhall with pious care lock up thy precious afhes. O! ARISTONÖUS ! ARISTONÖUS ! thou fhalt never die : thy memory fhall ever be imprinted on my heart. Sooner would I forget myfelf than fuch a friend, fo virtuous a man, fo bountiful a benefactor !

After this affectionate, tho' broken fpeech, SOPHRONYMUS performed the funeral rites, and placed the urn within his grandfire's

　　　　　monument.

monument. He facrificed whole hecatombs, whofe blood ran like a
torrent o'er the green-fwerd altars, which were raifed all round the
tomb. He poured forth large libations both of wine and milk.
He burnt perfumes imported from the diftant eaft, whofe odori-
ferous clouds curled upwards to the fkies. Forever after, by the
appointment of SOPHRONYMUS, annual funeral games were celebrated in remembrance of *Alcinus*, and his virtuous friend. Spec-
tators, in tribes innumerous, reforted thither from the fruitful
plains of *Caria*; from the delightful banks of the *Meander*, which
fports and plays along in many a winding wreath, and feems to quit
the country, which it waters, with reluctance; from the gay,
flow'ry banks of the *Cayftra*; from the fhores of rich *Pactolus*,
under whofe gentle waves roll golden fands; and from *Pamphylia*,
to which *Pomona*, *Ceres* and *Flora* ftrive who fhall be moft indulgent; in fine, from the extended plains of fair *Cilicia*, as a garden
watered with the torrent rolling impetuous down from *Taurus*,
whofe high head is ever filvered o'er with fnow. During thefe annual rites, the nymphs and fwains, dreft in loofe linnen robes,
white as the faireft lilies, fang the eulogiums of *Alcinus* and his
friend: there was no praifing the one without the other; nor could
they feparate two men, whofe union ftill cemented in the grave.

A miracle immediately fucceeded: on the firft day of celebration,
whilft SOPHRONYMUS was pouring forth his large libations both
of wine and milk, a myrtle of fragrant fmell, and beauteous verdure
fhot from the middle of the tomb; all on a fudden, reared its tufted
head, and with its interwoven boughs o'erfhadowed both the urns.
The whole affembly, with one voice, declared that ARISTONÖUS, as
a reward of his uncommon virtues, was by the Gods transformed
into this beauteous tree. SOPHRONYMUS, with pious care, watered
this myrtle himfelf; revered it as a God. It feemed to flourifh in
immortal youth; and, by this miracle, the Gods inftructed them
that *Virtue, which diffufes fuch perfumes upon the memories of men is
everlafting, and its own reward.*   F A B L E

FABLE II.

The ADVENTURES of MELESICHTON.

MELESICHTON was a native of *Megaris*, and a gentleman of an illuftrious family in *Greece*. When young, the heroic actions of his anceftors took up all his thoughts; and he gave early demonftrations of his courage and conduct, in feveral bold and ha-zardous engagements: but as he was too fond of grandeur, his high and expenfive way of living foon plunged him into a fea of troubles. He was obliged to fly with his wife PROXINÖE to a country-feat on the fea-fhore, where they lived together in a pro-found folitude. PROXINÖE was a lady highly efteemed for her wit, courage, and ftately deportment: many, who were in much better circumftances than MELESICHTON, made their addreffes to her on account of her birth and beauty; but true merit alone made him the object of her choice. Tho' their virtue and friendfhip were inviolable, tho' *Hymen* for many years had never united a happier pair; yet their mutual attachment and affection proved now but an aggravation of their forrows. MELESICHTON could have borne with lefs impatience the fevereft frowns of fortune, had he fuffered alone, or without fo tender a partner as PROXINÖE; and PROXINÖE with concern obferved, that her prefence augmented the pains of her MELESICHTON. Their fole comfort now arofe from the reflection that heaven had bleft them with two children, beauteous as the Graces: their fon's name was *Meliboeus*, and the daughter's *Poëminis*.

Meliboeus

Meliboeus was very active, ftrong, and courageous; in every gentle-
man-like exercife he excelled all the neighbouring youth. He
ranged around the forefts, and his arrows were as fatal and unerring
as thofe of *Apollo :* however, the arts and fciences—thofe nobler
rays of the deity—were more the objects of his contemplation,
than his bow was his diverfion. MELESICHTON, in his retirement,
laid before him all the advantages of a liberal education, and imprinted on his mind, betimes, the love of virtue and good manners.
Meliboeus, in his air and mien, was unaffected, foft and engaging;
yet his afpect was noble, bold, and commanded refpect. His father
caft his longing eyes upon him, and wept over him with a paternal
fondnefs. PÖEMINIS was by the mother inftructed with equal care,
in all the various arts with which the Goddefs *Minerva* has obliged
mankind; and to thofe ufeful accomplifhments were added the
charms of mufic : *Orpheus* never fung, or touched his lyre more
foftly than *Poëminis.* At firft fight fhe appeared like the young
Goddefs *Diana,* juft rifen from her native floating Ifland. Her
filver treffes were tied with a carelefs air behind ; whilft fome few
ringlets unconfined, played about her ivory neck at the breath of
every gentle zephyr. Her drefs was a thin loofe gown, tucked up
with a girdle, that fhe might move with the greater freedom.
Without the advantage of drefs, no nymph was ever fo beautiful,
fo free from pride, fo little confcious of her own charms. She was
never fo vain or curious as to examine her features in any tranfparent
ftream. The conduct and œconomy of the family was her whole
employment. But MELESICHTON, whofe thoughts were ever dark
and gloomy, whofe hopes of a return from his ftate of banifhment
were now all loft, fought every opportunity to be alone. The fight
of PROXINÖE and his children now aggravated his forrows : he
would often fteal out to the fea-fhore at the foot of a large rock,
full of tremendous caverns ; and there awhile bemoan his wayward
                                                    fate :

fate : from thence repair to a thick fhady vale, where—even at mid-day—no fun-beam ever entered. There would he fit on the margin of a purling ftream, and ruminate on all his ills. Soft, downy fleep ne'er clofed his weary eye-lids ; his words all terminated in fighs ; old age before his time had furrowed all his face ; and unable to bear the ftorm, he grew negligent of life, and funk under the weight of his misfortunes.

One day as he was reclined on a bank in his favourite, folitary vale, tired and fatigued with thought, he fell afleep ; and in a dream, faw the Goddefs *Ceres*, crowned with golden fheaves, who approached him with an air of majefty and fweetnefs :—" Why, MELESICH-" TON, faid fhe, art thou thus inconfolable ? Why art thou thus " overwhelmed with thy fate ?" " Alas! replied he, I am aban-" doned by my friends ; my eftate loft ; law-fuits and my creditors " forever perplex me ; the thoughts of my birth, and the figure " I have made in the world are all aggravations of my mifery ; and " to labor at the oar, like a galley-flave, for a bare fubfiftance, is " an act too mean, and what my fpirit never can comply with."

" Does nobility then, replied the Goddefs, confift in affluence " of fortune ?—No, MELESICHTON ; but in the heroic imitation " of thy virtuous anceftors: The juft man only is truly noble. " Nature is fufficed with a little : enjoy that little with the fweat " of thy brow : live free from dependance, and no man will be " nobler than thyfelf.—Luxury and falfe ambition are the ruin of " mankind.—If thou art deftitute of the conveniencies of life, who " fhould better fupply thee than thyfelf ? Be not terrified then at " the thought of attaining them by the fevereft induftry and ap-" plication ?"

She faid ; and immediately prefented him with a golden plough-fhare, and an horn of plenty. *Bacchus* next appeared, crowned with ivy, grafping his thyrfus in his hand, attended by *Pan*, playing on his rural pipe, while the fauns and fatyrs danced to the melodious mufic. *Pomona* next advanced, laden with fruits, and *Flora*, dreſt in all her gayeſt, fweeteſt flowers. In ſhort, all the rural deities caſt a favourable eye on MELESICHTON.

He waked, fully convinced of the application and moral ufe he ought to make of this celeftial dream. A dawn of comfort all on a ſudden ſhot thro' his foul, and he found new inclinations rife to the labours of the plain. He communicated his dream with pleafure to the fair PROXINÖE, who rejoiced with him, and approved of his interpretation. The next day they leſſened their retinue ; the valet and waiting-woman were immediately diſcharged, and all their equipage and grandeur at once refigned. PROXINÖE with *Poëmenis* fpun, while MELESICHTON and *Meliboeus* tended their ſheep,—— and at convenient hours weaved their own cloth and ſtuffs, and cut out and contrived every thing to the beſt advantage for themſelves and the reſt of the family. All their fine needle-works —in which *Minerva* herſelf could never be more curious—were now no more regarded ; and the glaring tent was refigned for the more advantageous diſtaff : their daily proviſions were the product of their own ground, and dreſt with their own hands. They milked their own kine, which now began to ſupply them with plenty. They purchafed nothing without doors. Every thing was got ready with decency and without hurry. Their food was fubftantial, plain, and natural ; and enjoyed with that true reliſh, which is infeparable from temperance and hard labour.

In this rural manner they lived, and every thing was neat and decent round about them ; all the coſtly tapiſtry was difpofed of ; yet the walls were perfectly white ; no part of the houfe in the leaſt diſorder : none of the goods foiled with duſt. The beds, tho' not of down, were clean, and proper for repofe. The very furniture of the kitchen—which you ſhall feldom find in great families—

was

was bright as filver; nothing ftood out of its proper place. At times of public entertainment PROXINÖE made the beft of paftry. She kept bees, whofe honey was fweeter than that which trickled from the trunks of oaks that grew in the golden age. Her cows made her willing prefents of large flowing bowls of milk. Her garden was plentifully ftored with variety of plants for fervice and delight, in their proper feafon; and by her peculiar induftry and fkill, fhe was the firft of all her neighbours that could produce them in perfection: her collection of flowers likewife was very curious; part of which fhe fold, after fhe had referved a fufficient quantity for the ornament of her houfe. *Pöeminis* trod in the fteps of her induftrious mother; fhe was ever chearful at her work, and fang as fhe went along to pen her fheep. No neighbour's flock could rival hers; no contagious diftemper, no rav'nous wolves durft ever approach them; her tender lambkins dance upon the plains to her melodious notes, whilft all the echoes round about with pleafure repeat the dying founds.

MELESICHTON tilled his own grounds, drove his own plough, fowed his feed, and reaped his harveft with his own hand. He is now fully convinced, that the hufbandman's life is lefs laborious, far more innocent and advantageous than the foldier's. No fooner had he cocked and got in his hay; but *Ceres*, with her yellow fruits, invited him to the field, and with large intereft repaid the debt fhe owed him. Soon after *Bacchus* fupplied him with nectar, worthy the table of the Gods. *Minerva* too complimented him with the fruit of her favourite, falutary tree. Winter was the feafon for repofe, when all the family met together were innnocently gay, and thankful to the Gods, for all their harmlefs unambitious pleafures: they ate no flefh, but at their facrifices, and their cattle never died but on their altars.

Meliboeus was thoughtful and fedate beyond his years. He took on himfelf the whole care and management of the larger cattle; hewed down large oaks in the forefts; dug aquaducts for the more commodious watering the meadows, and with indefatigable induftry

D   would

would eafe his father. His diverfions, at proper feafons, were hunting and courfing with the young gentlemen, his neighbours ; or im-
proving himfelf in his ftudies, of which Melesichton had laid the
folid foundation.

In a little time, Melesichton, by a life thus led in fimplicity
and innocence, was in better circumftances than at firft ; his houfe
was ftored with all the conveniences of life ; tho' there was nothing
in it ufelefs, or fuperfluous. The company he kept, for the moft
part, was within the compafs of his own family : they lived together in perfect love and harmony, and contributed to each others
happinefs. Their humble refidence was far from court, where pleafures bear fo high a price; their enjoyments were fweet, innocent,
eafy to be attained, and attended with no dangers in the purfuit.
Meliboeus and *Poeminis* were thus brought up, and inured to rural
labours : thus their former characters ferved only to infpire them
with greater courage, and make them eafy under the frowns of fortune. The encreafe of their ftock introduced no new and luxurious
courfe of life. Their diet was ftill as frugal as before, and their induftry continued with equal vigour. Melesichton's friends now
preffed him—fince fortune once again had proved propitious—to refume his former poft, and fhine again in the bufy world. To whom
he replied : " Shall I again give way to pride and luxury, the fatal
" caufe of all my late misfortunes ; or fhall I fpend my future days in
" rural labours, which have not only made me rich again, but what
" is more, compleatly happy ?"—To conclude,—one day he took a
tour to his old folitary fhade, where *Ceres* had thus kindly directed
his conduct in a dream, and repofed himfelf on the verdant grafs,
with as much ferenity of mind, as before with confufion and defpair.
There he flept again ; again the Goddefs *Ceres*, in the like gracious
manner, approached, and thus addreffed him. " True nobility,
" Melesichton, confifts in receiving no favours from any one,
" and beftowing them with a liberal hand on all.—Have your depen-
" dance on nothing but the fruitful bofom of the earth, and the works
" of your own hands. Never for luxury and empty fhew refign that
" folid good which is the natural, and inexhauftible fountain of true

F A B L E III.

A R I S T Æ U S AND V I R G I L.

VIRGIL, foon after his defcent to the infernal regions, came to the *Elyfian* fields; where the favourites of the Gods lived in perpetual blifs, on banks of never-dying flowers, amidft a thoufand little purling ftreams. The fhepherd ARISTÆUS, who was fitting amongft the Demy-gods, underftanding who he was, immediately approached, and thus addreffed him. The fight of fo divine a Poet as you are, is pleafure inexpreffible; Your verfes, fire, flow fofter than the dew upon the tender grafs ; fo fweet, fo harmonious are your numbers, they command our tears, and melt our hearts. Your tuneful fongs on me, and my bees, might make e'en *Homer* jealous. To you I ftand as much indebted for the honours that are paid me, as to the fun and to *Cyrene.* Not long ago I rehearfed fome beautiful paffages of yours to *Linus, Homer,* and *Hefiod.* No fooner had I finifhed, but all three drank large draughts of the river *Lethe* to forget them ; fo painful was the recollection of another's verfes, fweet as their own. The whole tribe of Poets, you know, are extremely jealous. Come, therefore, amongft them, and take poffeffion of your place.—Since they are fo partially jealous, as you obferve—replied VIRGIL—I fhall not be over-delighted with the place. I muft fpend many a tedious hour in fuch company ; for I perceive, like your bees, they prefently grow warm, and fhew their refentment. 'Tis true, replied ARISTÆUS, like bees, they buzz, and like them too have their ftings, and feek revenge on all that dare provoke them. There's another great man, I fee, fays VIRGIL, that I muft endeavour to oblige too, the divine *Orpheus,* I mean ;—pray do you live focially together?— I cannot fay we do, replied ARISTÆUS ; for he's as jealous of his wife, as the other three are of their compofitions. But you need not fear

a civil.

a civil reception there; for you have ufed him with abundance of good manners, and have been much more prudent, much more favourable than *Ovid*, in your relation of his quarrel with the *Thracian* dames, to whofe refentment he fell an unhappy victim. But we lofe time; let us enter this little facred grotto, watered with fo many fountains, clearer than the chryftal. Believe me, the whole facred band will rife, and pay their due refpects to you. Don't you already hear *Orpheus*'s tuneful lyre? and *Linus*, who fings the combat of the Gods againft the giants? Don't your hear *Homer* too, finging the heroic actions of the great *Achilles*; who flew the mighty *Hector*, to revenge the fall of his friend *Patroclus?* But *Hefiod* is the Poet, whofe difpleafure you have moft reafon to dread; for one of his fanguine complection will be apt to take diftafte at your admirable Treatife on Agriculture, which he imagines his peculiar province.

A RIST Æ US had no fooner finifhed his addrefs, but they arrived at the refrefhing fhades, where an eternal tranfport reigns, which infpires thefe mighty heroes. All rofe, and intreated V IRGIL to fit down, and repeat fome of his favourite verfes. At firft he fang low, with a becoming modefty; but at laft, grew bolder, and fpake with energy and tranfport. The moft jealous of them all, even againft their inclinations, were ravifhed at the mufic of his voice. *Orpheus*'s lyre, that had fo often charmed the very rocks and woods, now dropt out of his hand, and bitter tears flowed down his cheeks. *Homer* forgot the inimitable majefty of his Iliad, and the beauteous variety of his Odyffes. *Linus* miftook his flowing verfes for the compofition of his father *Apollo,* and at the ravifhing founds ftood fpeechlefs, and as immoveable as a ftatue. *Hefiod* himfelf could not refift fuch powerful charms. At laft, recollecting himfelf a little, he with much warmth and jealoufy thus addreffed him. O V IRGIL, thy works are more durable than monuments of brafs or marble! Yet ftill I prophefy the day will come, when a royal youth fhall tranflate them into his native language, and fhall fhare the honour with thee of having fung the conduct and œconomy of the bees.

FABLE

F A B L E IV.

The S T O R Y of A L I B E G the P E R S I A N.

CHA-ABBAS, King of *Perfia*, under pretence of taking a tour,
retired from court into the country, and concealed himfelf
under the character of a private gentleman, in order to take an unfufpected furvey of his fubjects in all their native innocence and
freedom. One favourite courtier alone had the honour to attend
him in his travels. " I have no right idea, fays the monarch to
" his companion, of the fimple, undifguifed manners of mankind.
" Courtiers act all in mafquerade. Crowned heads fee nothing of
" nature : every tranfaction is artifice and defign. I have a great
" inclination to pry into the fecret pleafures of a country life, and
" examine that part of my fubjects, who live retired, and neglected
" by the bufy world, and yet are in reality the props of my crown ✓
" and conftitution. 'Tis a pain inexpreffible to have none but fy-
" cophants about me, who embrace every opportunity, by their
" fulfome flatteries, if poffible, to betray me. My refolution, therefore,
" is fixed to vifit the fhepherds, and other fellow-labourers of the
" plains, to whom I fhall be a perfect ftranger." Thus determined,
he and his companion paft thro' feveral villages, where the nymphs
and fwains were affembled, to fpend the day in rural fports; and
his majefty was extremely pleafed to find fuch agreeable diverfions,
fo remote from court, fo innocent and inexpenfive. He dined in
one of their cottages, and having walked fomething farther than
ufual,

ufual, and created himfelf an appetite, their coarfe country diet proved a more agreeable entertainment than the vaft variety of coftly dainties at his own table. As he was walking over a meadow, enamelled with a thoufand various flowers, and watered with a clear, murmuring ftream, he fpied a young, gay fwain, reclined at the foot of a fhady elm, and playing on his rural pipe, whilft his tender flock ftood grazing round him, and liftened to his foft melodious notes. The monarch approached, looked earneftly at him, and was pleafed with his agreeable afpect, his eafy, unaffected air, which yet was graceful and majeftic. His fhepherd's drefs added new charms to his beauty. The King, at firft, fancied he was fome difcontented courtier in difguife; nor was convinced of his error, 'till the fhepherd told him his name was ALIBEG, and that all his relations lived in the adjacent village. Whilft his majefty propofed to him feveral queftions, he was exceedingly delighted with his pertinent and ready folutions. ALIBEG's eyes were lively and fparkling; but not in the leaft wild or roving: his voice foft, engaging and mufical. His features were fmall and beautiful; but not foft and effeminate. Tho' fixteen years of age, he had no idea of his own fuperior perfections. He imagined all his neighbours thought and talked as he did; and that nature had been as indulgent to them in their formation, as to himfelf.—Without the advantages of a liberal education, he directed his conduct by the dictates of right reafon. The King, after fome few familiarities, was charmed with his converfation. ALIBEG gave him a true and impartial account of the ftate and conftitution of the people; a fecret, Kings can never learn amidft a crowd of flatterers. Now and then his majefty would fmile at ALIBEG's expreffions, which were fo natural, fo open and unguarded. It was an agreeable novelty to the King to hear fuch free, fuch unftudied difcourfes. The monarch beckoned to his friend, and gave him private intimations not to

difcover

discover who he was, left ALIBEG, apprized of such a secret, should
be over-awed, and talk for the future with more referve; and so at
once lose all the beauties which freedom naturally gives to converfation.   I am now fully convinced, faid his majefty to his companion,
that nature appears as beautiful in the cottage as the palace. No
heir apparent to the crown feems nobler born than this youth,
who thus daily tends his harmlefs flock. How happy should
CHA-ABBAS be, had he a fon, fo beautiful, fo prudent, and fo much
the object of love and admiration ! In my opinion, he may be qualified for the higheft employments, and with proper inftruction may
become an able minifter of ftate. I'll take him home with me, and
give him a liberal education. The King accordingly at his return
took ALIBEG with him, as a new attendant,—ALIBEG was agree-
ably furprized to find his converfation had proved fo acceptable to a
monarch. Soon after their arrival, proper mafters were appointed,
firft to inftruct him in reading, writing, finging and dancing ; and
afterwards, in the feverer ftudies of the arts and fciences, which
cultivate the mind. At firft, the grandeur of a court made too
deep an impreffion on his heart, and his conftitution varied with his
advancement. His youth and reputation at court gave a new turn
to his judgment and moderation. He flung away his crook, his
pipe, and shepherd's weeds, and dreft himfelf in a purple veft richly
embroidered with gold ; he wore likewife a turbant on his head,
fet round with coftly jewels. The moft beautiful, the gayeft courtier, ferved only as a foil to ALIBEG. By induftry and application
he qualified himfelf for the moft important undertakings, and well
deferved the truft his mafter repofed in him ; who, fenfible of
ALIBEG's refined tafte for grandeur, and magnificence, made him
his jewel-keeper, or treafurer of his moft coftly furniture ; one of
the moft confiderable pofts in all *Perfia*.

During the whole reign of CHA-ABBAS, ALIBEG was a rifing
favourite :

favourite : but as he grew in years, he grew lefs gay, and often reflected with regret on his former happy ftate of life. " Happy
" days ! he would often whifper to himfelf, O days of innocence !
" Then were all my enjoyments chafte, attended with no dangers
" in the purfuit ! I never did, nor ever fhall fee days fo bleffed again.
" His majefty, by his royal bounty and munificence, has but undone
" me." Alibeg once more paid a vifit to his native village ; once
more obferved with curious eye, as he paffed along, where formerly
he danced and fang, and piped with his brother fwains. He made
feveral valuable prefents to his friends and relations round about ;
but advifed them, as they regarded their future welfare, to fhun the
dangers that attend ambition, and fpend their happy days in eafe
and innocence.

Alibeg, foon after the death of his indulgent mafter Cha-Abbas, was plunged in a fea of troubles. Cha-Sefi fucceeded his
father in the throne of *Perfia*. Some jealous, defigning courtiers
projected the downfal of Alibeg, and agreed to mifreprefent him
to the young monarch. They charged him as guilty of high crimes
and mifdemeanors ; with being falfe to the truft repofed in him by
the late King ; with clandeftinely difpofing of feveral rich moveables
in the treafury, and applying the fame to his own private ufe.
Cha-Sefi, afcending the throne of his father very young, was
perfectly credulous, regardlefs of right or wrong, and a prince of
but fmall penetration. However, he was fo vain as to imagine his
wifdom fuperior to his predeceffors, and that he could reform the
ftate. In order to remove Alibeg from his poft with fome colour
of juftice—purfuant to the advice of his envious council—he re-
quired him to produce forthwith the fcymitar, fet round with
coftly jewels, which his warlike grandfire always wore in the field
of battle. Cha-Abbas had formerly ordered all thofe jewels to be
removed ; and Alibeg brought indifputable proof of his innocence,
                                                                and

and of their being difpofed of, in obedience to the abfolute commands of his father, long before he had the honour of that important truft. When ALIBEG's enemies found this fcheme to ruin
him proved ineffectual, they prevailed on CHA-SEFI to oblige him
to produce an exact inventory of all the valuable furniture in the
treafury then in his cuftody, within fifteen days, on pain of difpleafure. Accordingly he did; and at the expiration of the term CHA-
SEFI was fo curious as to examine every individual article himfelf.
ALIBEG opened every clofet and cabinet, and concealed nothing that
was committed to his care. There was no one item miffing; the
office was every where clean, and in perfect order, and the regalia
clofely locked up in their proper repofitories. The young King
furprifed to find his treafury managed with fuch good conduct and
œconomy, had entertained a very favourable opinion of ALIBEG,
but that accidentally he obferved—at the end of a long gallery,
full of the richeft furniture—a private iron-door, on which were
three fubftantial locks. There, Sir, faid ALIBEG's accufers, whif-
pering him in the ear, there you'll find the royal plunder. CHA-
SEFI enraged, and looking fternly on ALIBEG, cried aloud, "This
" moment will I fee what is within thefe doors.—What have you
" concealed there?—I charge you fhew me." ALIBEG fell proftrate
at the King's feet, and implored his majefty, in the awful name of
the Gods, not to deprive him of all he valued upon earth.—" O!
" think! how unreafonable it is—fays he—at once to feize my laft
" referve for old age, after having ferved your royal father faithfully
" fo many years. Leave me but that; all that I have befides, I wil-
" lingly refign." CHA-SEFI now was fully convinced that ALIBEG
was guilty; and that there lay concealed the royal treafure. Now
more angry than before, and in louder terms, he demands the doors
to be unlocked. At laft ALIBEG produced the keys, and fmiling,
obeyed his orders. Upon examination, nothing was found but
ALIBEG's crook, his pipe, and the drefs he wore before his advance-

E   ment,

ment, which he frequently furveyed with pleafure, to remind him of his firft ftate of innocence. " Behold! faid he, O King, there lie " the valuable remains of my former felicity. It is not in the power " of your majefty, or fortune herfelf to take them from me. There, " royal Sir, is all the treafure I have referved to make me rich, " when your difpleafure fhall fink me into poverty. The reft I give " you back without regret ; leave your fervant but the dear pledges " of his firft happy ftation. Thefe, royal Sir, are durable riches ; " thefe never will deceive me. Riches ! that are natural, innocent, " and forever grateful to the wife man that lives content with the " conveniences of life, and fhuns the fatal charms of falfe ambition. " Riches! that are enjoyed without the lofs of liberty, and free " from dangers. Thefe never procured any man one moment's " difquiet. O! ye dear equipage of the plain, but happy man! " you only I admire ; with you I'll live and die. O! why was I " charmed with golden profpects that have deceived me, and ruined " my content! Here, O King, I freely refign all the favours your " goodnefs has conferred upon me. I'll only referve to myfelf what " I had, when firft your father faw me, and by his boundlefs libe- " rality undid me." The King, at the clofe of this addrefs, was fully convinced of ALIBEG's innocence and good conduct ; and fo far refented the villainy of his unjuft and envious accufers, that he banifhed them his court. ALIBEG foon after was made prime minifter ; and entrufted with the moft important affairs of the ftate ; however, every day he ftill furveyed his rural equipage, and kept them fafe in his repofitory to be ready at a time of need, whenever fickle fortune fhould again prove impropitious. He died in a good old age, without gratifying his revenge on his enemies, tho' in his power, and without laying up immenfe fums to enrich his pofterity. He left his relations but juft fufficient to maintain themfelves with credit in the ftation of fhepherds, a fituation of all others, in his opinion, moft free from care, and moft completely happy.

FABLE

FABLE V.

ROSIMOND AND BRAMINTES.

IN antient times, there was a youth, fair as the day, named ROSI-MOND, whofe virtue and good-humour were found equal to his beauty ; his elder brother BRAMINTES was his reverfe, and as much nature's difgrace, as ROSIMOND her mafter-piece. The younger was the mother's darling; the elder her averfion. BRAMINTES, jealous of her favours, invented a thoufand lies, if poffible to ruin ROSIMOND. He told his father, that his brother had contracted an inviolable friendfhip with a neighbour, who was his profeffed enemy ; that he revealed all the fecrets of the family ; and that they two concerted meafures by poifon to deftroy him. The father, alarmed at this impious accufation, treated ROSIMOND with the ut-moft inhumanity ; his cruelty extended even to blows that caufed the blood to gufh at every vein ; and then confined him to his chamber for three days fucceffively, without the leaft fubfiftence ; and at laft, drove him headlong from his doors, with dreadful im-precations that he would murder him the moment he returned. The mother, trembling at this ftrange feverity, durft not interpofe ; but fighed, and pitied his misfortunes. Poor ROSIMOND, thus difcarded, departs from home in a flood of tears; and knowing no friend that would receive him, in the evening traverfes a lonely wood. When night came on, he found himfelf at the foot of a large rock ;—at the entrance of one of the caverns, he laid himfelf down on a moffy bank, near which rolled gently a purling ftream,

E 2   and

and tired with thought, fell faft afleep. Soon as the dawning day appeared, he waked, and before his eyes—lo! a beauteous virgin ftood—dreft like *Diana*,—mounted on a grey courfer, whofe furniture was embroidered with gold. Pray, fhepherd, faid fhe, have you feen ftag or dogs pafs by this way? No, none at all—was his reply.—Friend, faid fhe, you look difconfolate—tell me your misfortunes freely.—Be comforted; behold! I here prefent you with a ring, which, if you ufe with difcretion, will make you the moft powerful, the moft happy man on earth. Turn but the diamond within your hand, and in a moment you'll be invifible. Turn it but without, and you'll be vifible again. When you fix it on your little finger, you'll perfonate the King's fon, attended by a numerous train of courtiers. Remove it again to your next, and you'll affume your proper fhape. The youth now underftood that his fair huntrefs was a fairy. Soon as fhe had thus revealed its fecret virtues, fhe ftruck into the grove. Rosimond refolves immediately to return home, and is impatient till he has made the experiment. He faw every tranfaction, and was privy to every fecret, without the leaft obfervance. Tho' he could have gratified his revenge, without difcovery, on his ungrateful brother; yet he only chofe to make himfelf known to his indulgent mother, with filial affection to embrace her, and tell her his ftrange adventure. Soon after this private interview, he put his magic ring on his little finger, and in a moment perfonated the young prince, followed by an hundred horfe-guards, and a numerous train of officers, all gayly dreffed. The father was confounded, to find his little cottage fo much honoured, and wholly at a lofs how to behave himfelf on fuch an unexpected vifit:—Pray, fays Rosimond, how many fons have you friend? Two, fir, replied the old man. Let me fee them, fays Rosimond: Call them to me this moment. I'll take them with me to court, and advance them according to their merit. The

conscious

confcious father, with hefitation, replied; This, fir, is my eldeft, with all fubmiffion, at your fervice. But where's your youngeft, fays ROSIMOND? I muft take him with me too. Sir, fays the old man, the unlucky lad is not at home. I correéted him fome time ago for his undutiful behaviour, and have never feen him fince. Severity, replied ROSIMOND, is a falfe ftep in education. Let your eldeft fon, however, follow me; go you, friend, along with my guards, who have my orders to take care of you. Two guards immediately conveyed the old man away; and the fame Fairy we mentioned before, meeting him in a foreft, ftruck him with her golden wand, drove him into a gloomy cave, and there confined him by her magic art. Do pennance there, faid fhe, 'till your injured fon fhall think proper to releafe you. In the mean time ROSIMOND went to court, foon after the young prince had embarked with proper forces for a diftant ifland, in hopes by conqueft to extend his father's empire; but being drove by adverfe winds upon an unknown coaft, his veffel bulged upon a rock, and he became the unhappy captive of the barbarous inhabitants. ROSIMOND appeared at court, as the King's fon, whom all imagined to be buried in the bofom of the ocean, and whofe untimely lofs was univerfally lamented. He pretended, that he had inevitably perifhed, had not fome friendly merchants took compaffion on his misfortunes, and preferved him. Joy fat on every face. The good old King folded his fon, whom he thought dead, within his eager arms, whilft tranfport ftopped the organs of his fpeech. The Queen received him with ftill fofter demonftrations of fondnefs and indulgence.—In fhort, the whole kingdom was engaged in public rejoicings on this happy occafion. One day, our imaginary prince thus befpoke his real brother. BRAMINTES, notwithftanding I have raifed you from the cottage to the palace; yet I know you bafe—ungenerous;—nay more, I know that by malicious mifreprefentations you have injured your

brother,

brother. He is now incognito at court. You ſhall ſee him ; and he ſhall have an opportunity to ſhew his juſt reſentment. Bra-mintes trembling with conſcious guilt, threw himſelf at the Prince's feet, and confeſſed his ingratitude. Notwithſtanding this ſub-miſſion, I charge you, ſpeak to your brother, and in the humbleſt manner ſolicit his pardon. 'Twill be an act of generoſity in him to grant it. You do not deſerve ſo much indulgence. He is now in my cloſet ; you ſhall have an interview immediately. In the mean time I'll withdraw to the next apartment, and leave you to yourſelves. Bramintes, in compliance with the prince's poſitive commands, attended in the cloſet. Immediately Rosimond re-aſſumed his ſhape, by virtue of his ring, and thro' a back door waited on his brother, who ſtood ſpeechleſs and confounded, when he firſt ſaw him. But ſoon recollecting himſelf, begged his pardon, with large promiſes of future love and friendſhip. Rosimond, with tears, embraced and forgave him. I have the honour, ſays he, to be the prince's peculiar favourite. Your liberty, your life is in my hands: but you ſhall find, tho' much you've wronged me, I'll be a brother ſtill. Bramintes, conſcious of guilt, with down-caſt eyes, and due ſubmiſſion, anſwered; but dared not claim the title of relation. Soon after Rosimond pretended to withdraw from court, and pay his addreſſes to a neighb'ring princeſs ; but his ſecret intention was to viſit his poor mother, to tell her minutely his tranſactions, and to preſent her with a ſmall purſe of gold, to ſup-ply her preſent occaſions. For tho' the King's treaſury was ever open to his demands ; yet he always uſed that boundleſs liberty, with amazing prudence and moderation. In the mean time the old King proclaimed war againſt a neighb'ring prince, on whoſe honour there could be no dependance. Rosimond went to the enemy's court, and by virtue of his magic ring, entered inviſibly into their moſt privy-councils. He improved all their ſchemes to

his

his own advantage. He got the ſtart of them, and broke all their meaſures; commanded the army againſt them; gained a compleat victory over them; and ſoon after ſettled an honourable peace, on the moſt advantageous terms. The King now determines to make a new alliance, by marrying his ſuppoſed victorious ſon, with a princeſs, fair as the Graces, and heireſs of a neighb'ring kingdom. But one day, ROSIMOND's guardian fairy, as he was hunting in the foreſt, where firſt ſhe met him, appeared to him a ſecond time. Preſume not, I charge you, ſays ſhe—with a ſolemn tone—to marry this royal beauty, in your aſſumed character. To deceive is mean and diſhonourable. The prince, whom you perſonate, ought in juſtice to fill in proper time his father's throne. Haſte then, and find him; he lies concealed in a far diſtant iſland : I'll be your guardian, and conduct your veſſel ſafe to port. Bid adieu to all the vanity of falſe ambition : be proud to ſerve ſo good a maſter, and, like an honeſt man, ſit down contented with your private ſtation. Theſe are my poſitive injunctions, and juſtice demands your obedience : Your neglect will raiſe my reſentment, and plunge you into all your former troubles. ROSIMOND readily complied with her wiſe advice. He embarked immediately, under colour of a private negotiation with a neighb'ring ſtate, and the partial winds ſoon wafted his veſſel to the deſtined ſhore. Our young prince was there the captive of the barbarous inhabitants, and employed to tend their cattle. The inviſible ROSIMOND ſoon found him in a diſtant meadow; and throwing his cloak, as inviſible as himſelf, over his ſhoulders, without the leaſt obſervance, reſtored him to his native freedom: They both ſet ſail together. New winds, obedient to the fairy's call, wafted them home. They ſoon arrived at the old King's apartment. ROSIMOND introduced the royal captive, and thus addreſſed his father. Your majeſty has hitherto imagined me to be your ſon; yet now I hold myſelf obliged to undeceive you : from my hands receive your royal heir. The King, greatly ſurprized, directed his diſcourſe to his real ſon. Was it not you, my ſon, who lately

triumphed

triumphed o'er our foes, and settled such a glorious peace ? Or hast thou, tell me true, been ship-wrecked on some distant coast, been taken by the savage brutes a captive, and dost thou owe thy life and liberty to this gracious youth ?—Yes, royal Sir, he generously came where I was made a slave :—it was he redeemed me : To him I am indebted for my restoration, and this happy meeting. To him, not me, belongs the honour due to your victorious arms. The King would have remained incredulous to his son's assertion ; but that ROSIMOND, by a new disposition of his ring, assumed the prince before him. The King was startled at the sudden metamorphosis, and knew not which to call his son. Not long after, the King would have loaded ROSIMOND with royal rewards for his distinguished love and loyalty ; all which he modestly refused, and only requested that his brother BRAMINTES might still be honoured with his favour. As for himself, he was fearful of the inconstancy of fortune, the frowns of an ill-natured world, and too conscious of his own demerits. He hoped, therefore, that his royal goodness would permit him to retire to his own country cottage, and spend the remainder of his days with his indulgent mother, in innocence and rural labours. The Fairy now met him a third time in the grove, shewed him the cavern where his father lay enchanted, and told him the proper magic terms that would release him. With filial piety he broke the charm. He waited with impatience for this opportunity of shewing his duty, and putting it in his father's power to spend his future days in peace and plenty. ROSIMOND, in short, was a generous benefactor to all his relations, and studied to do good for evil. Thus after his signal services for his King and country, the only favour that he requested, was the liberty to live retired, far from the reigning vices of the court. ROSIMOND wisely feared his magic gift might tempt him to resign his solitude, and make once more a figure in the busy world. He returned therefore to his favourite wood, and daily visited the happy cave, where first he saw his guardian-fairy, in hopes of the same honour once again. In a

short

short time, she obliged him with her presence ; and he, with mo-
desty, returned her magic ring. " Here, madam, says he, I thank-
" fully restore you back your ineftimable, tho' dangerous present—
" which, unless with prudence used, must soon prove fatal to its
" owner. I durst not trust to my own conduct, whilst I have it in
" my power to quit my rural innocence, and gratify at pleasure
" lawless passions."

Whilst Rosimond was thus refigning all his grandeur, Bramintes, still as ungenerous, still as vicious as before, endeavoured,
by false insinuations to prevail on the young prince, now in possession
of his father's throne, to humble Rosimond. Your brother—says
the Fairy to Rosimond—is incorrigible ; he aims to bring your
past conduct into question, and undo you. No punishment is equal
to his demerits. His fate is sealed.—I'll go this moment, and give
him this ring, which you have refigned. Rosimond, reflecting on
the fatal consequence—wept. Then, turning to the Fairy : What
horrid punishment, said he, will such a dangerous present be to him ?
He will then rule absolute, and every honest man will fall a victim
to his power. Your remark is just—replied the Fairy.—The same
medicine may be applied with good effect to one constitution, that
will infallibly destroy another. The profperity of the wicked is the
sure foundation of all their future miseries. The villain, flushed with
arbitrary power, like *Phaëton*, drives headlong to his ruin.—She va-
nished ; and in the form of an old tattered beggar, appeared at court,
when meeting the gay Bramintes, she thus addressed him. " The
" ring, sir, which I gave your brother, and by which alone he raised
" his fortune, is once again in my difpofal. For you I have referved
" the valuable present ; be cautious of the power it gives you."
Bramintes, smiling, replied ; " My brother's conduct shall be no
" rule to me ; I ne'er shall fearch, like him, through foreign climes,
" to find an heir, when I can fill the throne myfelf." Bramintes,
invested with this magic ring, pries into every private family's concerns, acts every day the traitor ; betrays the councels of his master,
plunders his subjects, drinks deep of fenfual pleafures, and makes even

F

murder

murder his diverſion. His crimes, tho' inviſible, ſtartled all mankind.
The King could not imagine which way his ſecrets could be made
ſo public ; but the pride and boundleſs profuſion of BRAMINTES
gave room for ſuſpicion that his brother's ring was now in his poſ-
ſeſſion.   A foreigner, ſubjećt to a prince of an enemy nation, was employed, by high bribes, to make the diſcovery.   This hireling went
accordingly to BRAMINTES one night, and made him an offer, in
the name of his maſter, of vaſt ſums of money, and other demon-
ſtrations of friendſhip, if he, by proper ſpies, would give him ſecret
intelligence of what paſt at court.   BRAMINTES accepted of the
terms, and met at the place appointed ; where he received a large
gratuity as an encouragement to purſue ſo important an undertaking.
Amongſt other exaltations of his own merit, he made his boaſt of his
inviſible ring.   The next day, he was taken into cuſtody by one of
the King's meſſengers.   The ring, and ſeveral treaſonable papers
were found upon him, which were undeniable evidences of his guilt.
—ROSIMOND made all the intereſt at court he poſſibly could, to ſave
his life, but to no purpoſe.   BRAMINTES was executed as a
traitor ; and thus his magic ring proved a greater curſe to him, than
before it had been a bleſſing to his brother.

The King, to make ROSIMOND ſome recompence for the loſs of
ſo near a relation, returned him his ring, as a treaſure of ineſtimable
value.   The diſconſolate ROSIMOND was of another opinion.   He
went again to the grove, to find out his guardian Fairy.   Here, madam, ſays he, once more take back your ring.   My brother's fate is
now a full convićtion of the truth you told me, tho' before, I could not
rightly comprehend you.   Take back the fatal cauſe of my unhappy
brother's death.   He might, alas ! have ſtill been living, and not have
brought down his poor parents grey hairs with ſorrow to the grave.
He might, alas ! have ſtill been wiſe, have ſtill been happy, had his
unruly paſſions been confined.   O ! how dangerous is the gift of
power ! Take back your fatal ring.   Unhappy is the man who next
enjoys it.   I only beg this boon, that when you part with it again it
may not be beſtowed on any friend of ROSIMONDS.

F A B L E VI.

The ADVENTURES of FLORISA.

A Poor country-woman had contracted an intimate friendſhip with a Fairy. It happened the good woman was brought to bed of a daughter, and the Fairy was invited as a favourite gueſt on that joyful occaſion. She came accordingly ; and as the infant lay in her arms, ſhe thus beſpoke the mother. " Make your own free " choice, my friend ; this daughter of yours, if you requeſt it, ſhall " be fair as the new-born day ; the beauties of her mind ſhall ſtill " be more conſpicuous than her perſonal charms ; ſhe ſhall in time " be a powerful princeſs ; but very unfortunate ; or—ſhe ſhall make " no figure in the world, be a plain, honeſt country-woman, like " yourſelf ; but live at eaſe, contented with that little portion which " the Gods allot her."—The ambitious country-woman was ſoon determined in her choice. " Give my daughter wiſdom, beauty, " and a crown, ſhe ſaid, at all adventures." All on a ſudden, young cupids dance in her eyes, and her virgin-charms become the object of envy and admiration. Her behaviour is affable, ſweet and en-gaging ; her apprehenſion quick and lively ; whatever accompliſh-ments ſhe ſtudied, ſhe attained them to the utmoſt degree of perfec-tion. When ſhe danced on any public feſtival upon the verdant plain, her movement was inimitably graceful. Her voice was ſweeter than the lyre of *Orpheus*, and her airs were chiefly her own compoſures. At firſt, ſhe was all artleſs innocence ; but as ſhe was playing on the margin of a tranſparent ſpring, ſhe gazed with

admiration

admiration on her beauteous form; and with a secret pride observed the partial hand of nature. Whole crouds would stand in ranks to see her pass along, which made her still more conscious of her charms. The mother, relying on the friendship and foreknowledge of the Fairy, viewed her child with partial eyes, traced the distant princess in every little action, and almost spoiled her by excess of fondness. The virgin-beauty now would neither spin, nor sew, nor tend her sheep; but either range thro' all the meads, collect the gayest flowers, and artfully dispose them in her dress; or walk, and sing, and dance, beneath the sylvan shades. The King of the country where she lived was a very powerful prince, and determined to marry his only son, whose name was Rosimond, as soon as prudence would permit. He would hearken, however, to no proposals of alliance with any of the neighb'ring states, having been foretold by a Fairy, that he should one day see a nymph more beauteous, more accomplished than the gayest princess. He resolved, therefore, to summon all the country-virgins throughout his kingdom, who were under eighteen years of age, forthwith to repair to court, for his review and final choice. A thousand moderate beauties attended on this occasion. But thirty—to whom nature had been peculiarly indulgent—were soon distinguished from the croud. Florisa—for that was the name of our enchanted beauty—procured the favour, without solicitation, to be introduced amongst this happy number. These thirty rural beauties were conducted into one of his majesty's most spacious halls; and there ranged in an amphitheatrical form, that the King and his son might survey them all at once in a proper light. Florisa, at first glance, appeared, amidst these candidates for beauty, like the fairest spring-flower in a bed of marygolds, or an orange-tree, in all its glory, amidst a row of brambles. The King, without hesitation, declared Florisa princess: Rosimond too thought himself happy in his father's choice. Florisa now resigns

her

her rural habit for royal robes, embroidered thick with gold. A thoufand coftly jewels glitter round about her. A large train of attendants wait upon her will. Happy is the lady that can ftudy what will pleafe her beft, and fave her even the pain of thought. A magnificent apartment was fitted up for her reception ; the rooms were lined round with coftly looking-glafs, inftead of tapiftry hangings, that turn which way fhe would, with pleafure fhe might fee her charms reflected , and that the prince, where'er he caft his eyes, with tranfport might adore them. Hunting, gaming, and the thoufand other entertainments of the court, were no amufements now to Rosimond. All his pleafure centered in her charming con-verfation : and, as the old King his father died foon after *Hymen* had confirmed their joys, Florisa fulfilled the Fairy's prediction, reigned as Queen, and by her good conduct, and peculiar penetra-tion, fettled the moft important affairs of ftate with univerfal ap-plaufe. *Chronipota*, the old Queen, whofe temper was fubtle, ill-na-tured and malicious, grew jealous of Florisa ; thro' the de-fects of nature and age together, fhe looked like a very fury. The charms of Florisa did but fet her deformity in a more glaring light, and provoked her to the laft degree. The reflection that fhe was only a foil to Florisa was a pain infupportable. She was con-fcious of Florisa's prudence and good conduct ; and therefore abandoned herfelf to all the outrages of malice and revenge. " Are " not you, fhe would often fay to her fon, an abject, poor-fpirited " prince, thus to wed an obfcure country-lafs, and fet her up for " a Goddefs ? One too, that's as proud and imperious, as if fhe was " heirefs to a throne. When your royal father thought of fuch a " fettlement, he made me the object of his choice, as I was " daughter to a King, equal with him in glory. Thou fhouldft " poor, unambitious boy, have traced his foot-fteps. Send back, for

" fhame,

" fhame, your fylvan Goddefs to her fhady groves : Act like a King,
" and take fome princefs to your arms, whofe birth and character
" deferve the blefling." As Rosimond, however, was deaf to her
reproofs. The inveterate *Chronipota*, to fatiate her revenge, one
day intercepted a letter which Florisa had wrote, in the moft tender terms, a heart full of love and gratitude could conceive to her
royal mafter : this letter the fury gave to a young courtier, one
of her creatures, and enjoined him, on pain of her difpleafure, to
own the contents directed to himfelf, to lay it before his majefty
with all the tokens of a loyal refentment, and to fet Florisa's
inconftancy and falfhood in the moft odious light. Rosimond, in
the hurry and confufion of a jealous thought, and exafperated by
his mother's pernicious counfels, ordered Florisa to be clofe confined for life, within a high tower, built on the fummit of a rock,
that bellied o'er the fea. There fhe fat whole nights and days in
floods of forrow, unable to conceive what fhe had done to merit
fuch inhuman treatment. No one was allowed to attend her, but
an old confident of *Chronipota*'s, who was inftructed to infult her,
and triumph over her misfortunes. Florisa now reflected on her
once happy ftate of life, her humble birth, and all her harmlefs
rural entertainments. One day, as fhe was drowned in tears, de-
ploring her ambitious mother's fatal choice, her old tormentor came
to tell her that the King's officer attended to behead her; and that
death alone could make atonement for her crimes. Death, faid
Florisa, to a wretch like me, is welcome.—I am prepared.—
The officer, in fhort, thro' the mifreprefentations of old *Chronipota*,
ftood ready, with his fword drawn, to execute the King's com-
miflion; when, on a fudden, a lady, richly dreffed, appeared, and
flopped the impending blow; afferting that fhe came from court,
with pofitive injunctions to deliver a private meffage to the dying
Queen.

Queen. Her old fury of a guardian readily acquiefced with thefe pretended orders, not doubting but the lady was one of *Chroni-pota's* retinue; but, in reality, fhe was the Fairy in difguife, who had foretold FLORISA's troubles. After having ordered every perfon to withdraw, fhe thus addreffed her. " Are you wil-" ling to refign your beauty, which has proved your ruin?—Will " you renounce your title to a crown, refume your rural drefs, and " return to your former humble fituation?" — With tranfport FLORISA accepted the propofal. Here, put on, fays the Fairy, this enchanted mafk. On the firft application, her features began to extend, and grow in difproportion. She now feems the difgrace, as before, fhe appeared the pride of nature. Thus metamorphofed, it was impoffible to know her; and fhe paffed unfufpected thro' the guards, who were ordered to be fpectators of her execution. She followed the Fairy; and under her convoy arrived fafe in her own country. Strict fearch is now made all over the tower for the unhappy beauty, but to no purpofe. The news of this miraculous efcape was related, with the utmoft furprize to the King and to *Chronipota*; who iffued out frefh orders throughout the kingdom, but in vain, for her reprizal. The Fairy delivered her fafe into her mother's hands, who had never known her daughter, had fhe not been before apprized of her transformation. FLORISA was very well contented to return to her former ftation, to be deformed, and live in obfcurity in the country, where all her bufinefs was to tend her fheep. A day fcarce paft, but what fhe heard her tale related, and her fall deplored. Her adventures, in fhort, were the fubject of a thoufand fongs fo moving they commanded tears. With pleafure fhe would fit, and fweetly fing thofe fongs herfelf, and weep with her companions: but thought herfelf more happy now than ever, and to her dying day retained the fecret.

FABLE

F A B L E VII.

The History of ALFAROUTE and CLARIFILIA.

ONce on a time there was a King, named ALFAROUTE, who was the delight of his fubjects, and the terror of all his enemies. He was a wife and good prince, juft, valiant, and active; deficient in no royal qualification. A Fairy, one day in private told him, that fome unforefeen misfortunes would attend him, unlefs he prevented them, by virtue of a magic ring, which fhe put upon his finger. When he turned the diamond within his hand, he became immediately invifible; and the moment he turned it without, became vifible again. This ring proved of fingular fervice to him, and was his favourite recreation. On the leaft miftruft of any ill-projecting fubject, by virtue of his ring, he was prefent with him in his moft fecret retirements, and knew all his domeftic concerns without the leaft obfervance. If he was apprehenfive of an invafion from abroad, he fat amidft their privy councils undifcovered. Thus he baffled with pleafure all the projects that were formed to fow diffentions amongft his people; found out all the plots and confpiracies, tho' ne'er fo clofely laid, againft his perfon; and difconcerted all the meafures of thofe, who would gladly fubvert his conftitution. This indulgence, however, of the Fairy's, did not anfwer all the ends of his ambition: he begged a more extenfive power ftill; and wifhed, that by virtue of his ring, he could tranfport himfelf to diftant regions in a moment. The Fairy, fighing,

replied;

fo captivating a beauty :—But jealoufy, that pois'nous paffion, found
a paffage to his breaft, to interrupt the current of his joys. His eyes
invifibly were ever on her, obfervant of her private conduct ; yet
ftill he found her chafte, the worthy object of his love and admiration. Still there remains fome fmall diftruft behind, which gives
him anxious pain. The Fairy, who had foretold the fatal confe-
quence that would attend his laft requeft, whifpered her cautions in
his ear fo often, that he deemed her impertinent. Exprefs orders
were immediately given, that fhe fhould leave the court ; and the
Queen herfelf was inftructed, on pain of his difpleafure, never to
fee her more. Her majefty, with great reluctance, complies with
this fevere injunction ; for the Fairy was her much refpected friend
and favourite. One day, the Fairy, defirous to inform the Queen
of fome material occurrences, affumed the fhape of one of her officers, and under that difguife, with eafe gained admittance into her
private apartment, where, with pleafure, fhe difcovered who fhe was.
The Queen flew into her arms with a true lover's fondnefs. The
King, who at the fame time was there invifible, and faw their tender embraces, burned with fury and indignation. He drew his
fword, in the height of his refentment, and plunged it in the bofom of the guiltlefs Queen. That moment the Fairy reaffumed her
proper fhape.—Inftantaneoufly the King perceived his fatal error,
and confeffed his CLARIFILIA virtuous.—ALFAROUTE would fain
have fallen upon his fword to make atonement. The Fairy inter-
pofed, and ftrove to mitigate his forrows. The Queen, as fhe lay
weltring in her blood, and juft expiring, faintly faid.—" O! AL-
" FAROUTE, tho' by thy cruel hand I die, I die thy ever faithful,
" loving wife." The King now mourned his wayward fate, and
his own rafh requeft. He returned the fatal magic ring, and begged
the Fairy to retake his wings. The remnant of his days he fpent in
gloomy thoughts and in excefs of forrow. The only mitigation of
his grief was once a day to vifit CLARIFILIA's tomb, and bath it
with his tears. ·   F A B L E

FABLE VIII.

The STORY of the Old QUEEN and PERONELLA.

IN days of yore, there was a QUEEN so very antient, that her gums were all unarmed, and her forehead as bald, as an old barren plain. Her head tottered, as the aspen leaf trembles, when ruffled by the wind. Her eyes were dim, and sunk within their sockets. Her visage was all rough, unfeatured, and deformed. She was lower in stature by one-half than in her youth; she grew globular, and her mountain-back was so high, that any one might justly think she had been crooked from her cradle. A Fairy, who was present at her mother's labour, approached, and thus addressed her. " Have you an inclination to renew your youth? I should " be proud, replied the QUEEN, of so valuable a blessing. All, all " my costly jewels, I'd resign with pleasure to be but twenty-one " again." Then, says the Fairy, we must find some proper person, who will assume your age, and willingly transfer her health and youth to you. On whom shall we bestow your hundred years ?— Immediate search was made, by the QUEEN's orders, for such proper person, as would gladly accept of the exchange. A crowd of beggars first surround the palace, and offer to be old, upon condition to be rich ; but when they beheld her rueful face, her ropy chain of rheums, and all the thousand ills that hovered round her, they looked upon her with an eye of pity, despised the proffer, and rather chose to beg in rags from door to door. Others, with vain,

ambitious

ambitious thoughts infpired, drew near the throne, to whom fhe made large promifes of titles and preferments; but, at the fight of her, they cried; honour is an empty name without enjoyment. How fhould we blufh to ftir abroad, fo hideous and deformed!—At length, a country lafs, named PERONELLA, fair as *Aurora*, ftood before the QUEEN, and for the crown itfelf, propofed the refignation of her youthful bloom. The wrinkled QUEEN at firft brow-beats the virgin for her high demands: but to no purpofe; young fhe muft be again, at all adventures. " No, no, the QUEEN replied, " the crown fhall be divided, and we'll fhare it equally between us. " Sure that's reward fufficient for a girl like thee!" " Boldly the " maid replied, 'tis not fufficient. The crown is mine or your's; " I'll ftill retain my poverty and blooming youth, keep you your " kingdom and your hundred years, with all its train of ills, and " death itfelf behind them." " But, fays the QUEEN, what fhall " I do, when I've refigned my crown?" " Be gay, and fing, and " dance as I do now, fays PERONELLA:—then practifed all before " her." The QUEEN, whofe feeble knees knocked one againft another, replied, " And how will you behave yourfelf when once " my throne is yours? you are a ftranger to the cares of age." " I " don't well know, fays PERONELLA; but I'll make the beft ufe of " it I can: I have an unaccountable inclination to try the experi- " ment, for I have heard 'tis a moft glorious thing to be a QUEEN." Whilft the QUEEN and PERONELLA were thus fettling the pur- chafe, in came the Fairy, and thus befpoke the country-maid. " Are you willing to be made like to this old QUEEN, and try whe- " ther her ftate will be an agreeable exchange to you?" " I am, " fays PERONELLA." Immediately her leathern face fits all in wrinkles; all hoary are her hairs; fhe frets; fhe fcolds; her crazy noddle totters, and her fhrivelled checks hang down beneath her jaws; her age is now five fcore. The Fairy opens a little box, and

out-ftarts

out-ftarts a regular band of officers and courtiers, richly drefled, who grew to their full ftature as they marched, and paid their proper homage to the new-made QUEEN. They prepare a fplendid entertainment for her reception. But fhe has no appetite for all their dainties, nor could fhe tafte them if fhe had. She blufhes, and fits in pain; fhe knows not what to fay, or do. She coughs, 'till fhe is juft expiring; fhe dribbles on her chin; a watery drop hangs on her fhrivelled nofe, which fhe difcharges with her fleeve. She peers into the looking-glafs, and finds her features more wrinkled than an old grandame's ape. On the other hand, the late QUEEN ftood, fmiling in a corner: her eyes began to fparkle, and her limbs to feel new life. Her hair grew beautifully black, her teeth, like ivory, white; her complection ruddy as the blufhing rofe; and her old crooked form rifes by flow degrees as upright as an arrow. But fhe was grown a perfect flattern; and tho' her petticoats hung only half-way down her legs; yet they were dirty, and as draggled as a beggars. This was an odd equipage to her; and the guards, fuppofing her to be no other than fome common fcullion, would have drove her headlong out of court. Then PERONELLA thus befpoke the QUEEN. "We neither of us, I find, "live in our proper element.—Take you your crown again; give "me my rural drefs." That moment the exchange was made. The QUEEN grew old again, and PERONELLA young. So fickle is a female mind, they both again repented, but too late. The Fairy now had doomed them irrecoverably to their proper ftations. Every day the fuperannuated QUEEN would weep; and, under the preffure of every diforder, cry, alas! "Was I now PERONELLA, I fhould "lodge, indeed, in a poor, humble cottage, with cheftnuts for my "food, inftead of dainties; but then I fhould divert myfelf "amongft my fellow-fwains, in dancing to their tuneful notes be- "neath the fylvan fhades. What are foft beds of down to me, "whofe

" whofe eye-lids never clofe in gentle flumbers ? or crouds attend-
" ing round me, when I die with pain ?" Thefe melancholy reflections made her ever reftlefs and impatient ; and twenty-four
phyficians, who continually attended her, added new fewel to the
flame. In fhort, in about two months time, death ended all her
woes. PERONELLA was dancing with her companions, on the
margin of a purling ftream, when firft fhe heard the mournful news;
and then fhe was convinced her happinefs was owing more to
fortune, than her own good conduct. Not long after, the Fairy
came again to PERONELLA, and offered three hufbands to her
choice. The firft, old, peevifh, difagreeable, jealous, and ill-natured ; but rich, of an illuftrious family; and one, who, neither
night or day, would let her ftir one moment from him. The fecond, very handfome, good-natured, obliging, of an antient and
honourable race ; but poor, and unfuccefsful in all his undertakings. The laft, a country-man, neither handfome, nor difagreeable ; one, who would neither doat upon her, nor abufe her ; one,
in fhort, who was neither very neceflitous, nor yet abounding.
PERONELLA was at a lofs to make her choice ; for fhe was naturally
fond of drefs, of grandeur and magnificence. " You are ftill a
" filly girl, I find, fays the Fairy, you don't know your own ad-
" vantage. The country-man is your bridegroom if you're wife.
" You yourfelf would be too indulgent to the fecond ; the firft
" would doat on you : in either of their arms you'd be unhappy.
" The third would never ufe you ill : fit down contented with that
" thought ; 'tis better far to dance upon the fern, or verdant grafs,
" than in a palace ;—and to be the poor contented PERONELLA
" in a cottage, than the gay fafhionable lady, furrounded with a
" thoufand cares. If you can bid adieu to all the vanity of falfe
" ambition, you and your fhepherd may be truly happy."

FABLE

FABLE IX.

L Y C O N.

WHEN *Fame* had, with her brazen trump, proclaimed aloud to all the rural deities, and *Cynthian* fwains, that LYCON would forfake them, a melancholy murmur filled the fhady groves. Echo, and all the adjacent vales repeat the mournful founds. The rural pipe, the flute and haut-boy, are now heard no more. The fhepherds, in excefs of forrow, break their reeds. All nature languifhes with fympathetic woe. The trees hang down their drooping heads, and lofe their verdure. Till then the face of Heav'n was all ferene; but now obfcured with clouds. Now the bleak north-wind uncloaths the meadows, and difrobes the groves, as at the approach of winter. The rural Deities themfelves bemoan their lofs. The Dryads quit their hollow oaks, and figh for LYCON. The mournful Deities affemble now beneath a lofty tree whofe fummit reached the fky; whofe wide-extended arms for ages paft had covered its old mother earth. The fylvan nymphs that ufed to entertain themfelves with dances, fongs, and other harmlefs fports, around this knotty, cumb'rous tree; now met, alas! to drop their tears, and tell their melancholy tale. O! we fhall never fee dear LYCON more, they cry; the dear, dear object of our wifhes flies our groves!—Too cruel fate thus to remove him from us!—Thrice happy grove, which he fhall honour with his prefence!—Now we fhall hear his tuneful voice no more; no more behold him bend his bow, and with his arrows, unerring as *Apollo's*, wound the feathered game. Great *Pan* himfelf refigns his flute; the fauns and

fatyrs

fatyrs too fufpend their dances to join the melancholy wood-nymphs. The little harmlefs birds fit drooping on the boughs, and quite forget their fongs. Only the folitary fcreech-owl and the ill-boding birds, with their ear-wounding notes, difturb the filence of the groves. Sweet *Philomela*, with her tuneful choir, now ceafe their warbling ftrains. All on a fudden, *Flora* and *Pomona*, hand in hand, appear within the center of the grove; fmiles fit upon their faces, glowing celeftial red : the former wore a chaplet of rofes on her head, whilft prim-rofes and violets fprang up beneath her feet : the latter grafped within her hand a horn of plenty, filled with au-tumnal fruits, the grateful earth's return for the kind labours of the fwain. Be comforted—they cried to the diftreffed affembly—tho' LYCON will, indeed, your groves forfake; yet ftill he flies no far-ther than the mountain confecrated to the God *Apollo*. There you fhall fee him cultivate our happy gardens. With his own hands, he there fhall plant green trees ; delicious roots for man's fupport, and fragrant flowers for his amufement. Ceafe, ceafe, O north-wind, with your poifonous blafts to ruffle LYCON's favourite gardens. Be kind to LYCON, who fhall prefer his rural entertainments be-fore the luxury of courts; fhall love this happy fituation, and leave it with reluctance. No fooner had they fpoke, but forrow turned to joy : the fubject of their fongs was their loved LYCON's praife. He will, they cry, delight in gardens, as *Apollo*, when fhepherd to *Admetus*, loved his flocks. A thoufand foft celeftial fongs filled all the grove, and LYCON's favourite name refounded from the foreft to the diftant hills. The fhepherds, with their tuneful pipes, re-peat the pleafing founds. The birds too, on the fhady boughs, in their own language, warble out the name of LYCON. Nature is decked in all her pride ; the trees are cloathed with fruits, the fields with flowers: The gardens, that wait for his return, boaft all the

II

beauties

beauties of the spring, and the gay gifts of autumn. The very diftant looks of Lycon round the mountain have a magic power, and
make it fruitful there, when he has rooted up its numerous weeds
and barren plants, he shall collect the olive and the myrtle, and
wait with patience till the God of war directs him where to pluck
the laurel.

F A B L E

FABLE X.

A Compliment to a Young PRINCE, after an ill Night's Reft.

PHOEBUS, having traverfed the expanfe of Heaven, and run his deftined round, plunged deep his fiery courfers into the hefperian waves. The horizon was bordered round with purple ; the fky feemed all inflamed with the bright tracks of light, the God had left behind him. The fcorching dog-ftar parched up the thirfty plain. The plants loft all their verdure, and languifhed for the dews. The fading flowers hung down their drooping heads ; nor could their feeble ftalks fupport their weight. The very zephyrs witheld their gentle breezes. The air, which all things living breathed, was fuffocating, clofe and fultry. Night, with her cool, refrefhing fhades, could not allay the exceffive heat ; nor fhed thofe balmy dews on the laborious and dejected fwains, which, in the common courfe of nature, fhe diftils, when the ftars fhine, and *Hefper* twinkles bright behind them ; nor had her crop of poppies power to charm to reft the languifhing creation. *Phœbus* alone, reclining on the foft bofom of his beauteous *Thetis*, flept at eafe. But when he waked, when the officious hours had got his chariot ready, and *Aurora* had begun her rofy progrefs, he difcerned the face of Heaven all over-fpread with clouds ; faw the wild wafte, the ruins of the ftorm, which had the night before affrighted all the lower world. From the damp earth the infectious vapours rofe, which added flame to the red lightning's flafh, and horror to the

H 2   thunder.

thunder. The boifterous winds, with hideous roar, burft from their ftony caverns; the mountain-grounds fmoked with the hafty rains, which rolled in torrents down upon the vallies. The golden fun, who, with his beams magnetic, warms the world, faw as he rofe new devaftations with concern; but with fuperior grief, beheld a youth, the darling of the Mufes, his own peculiar favourite, robbed of his repofe by this impetuous ftorm, foon as the dew of fleep had fallen upon him, and with foft, flumberous weight, inclined his eye-lids. The indulgent God was thinking to drive backwards, and retard the day to recompenfe his lofs. My darling ftill, he cried, fhall fleep. Still fleep fhall feal his eyes, and hufh his cares, renew his health and ftrength, that he may imitate the great *Alcides*, and add a fweetnefs to his difpofition not to be expreffed, the only virtue that he poffibly can want. If he fleeps found and laughs; foftens his temper, and delights in play; if he but loves mankind, and ftudies to be loved, the various graces will unite, and form the man compleat.

F A B L E

F A B L E XI.

Young B A C C H U S and the Critic F A U N.

ONE day, young Bacchus, pupil to *Silenus*, was diverting himfelf with the Mufes in a grove, whofe folemn filence never was difturbed, but by the murmurs of foft, purling ftreams, and the fweet harmony of warbling birds. So thick and gloomy were the verdant fhades, *Apollo's* brighteft beams could never pierce them. The beauteous fon of *Semele*, as he was ftudying the lan-guage of the Gods, fat at the foot of an old fhady oak, whofe fa-cred trunk was pregnant in the golden age with men. The oracles of old from thence were given ; there ftill it ftood, and flourifhed in immortal youth. Behind this hollowed oak, a brifk, young Faun, unfeen, ftood liftning to the verfes which the God repeated, and with a fcornful air, whifpered each little error to *Silenus*. At fome fmall diftance the *Naïades* and rural nymphs ftood fmiling. Young was the critic, wanton and genteel. His head was dreft with ivy mixed with vine-leaves. Clufters of grapes adorned his temples. Over his left fhoulder hung a curious fcarf, compofed of ivy wreathed ; and the young God was pleafed to fee his favourite leaves. From the girdle downwards, the Faun was dreffed in a tremendous lion's fkin, the trophies of his conqueft in the foreft. In his hand he grafped a knotty fheep-hook. He waved his tail, in many a wanton wreath upon his back. But as the God no longer could endure this bold, infulting critic, who cenfured the leaft word irregularly placed, with a ftern look, and haughty tone, he cried : " How durft thou, " faucy Faun, remark thus on the fon of *Jove?*" The Faun, un-daunted, with a fmile, replied : " How can the fon of *Jove* commit " fuch blunders ?"

F A B L E

FABLE XII.

The NIGHTINGALE and LINNET.

ON the ever verdant banks of the river *Alpheus* ſtands a grove, where the *Naïades* diffuſe their noiſy waters, and refreſh the new-born flowers. The Graces often bathe themſelves in theſe chryſtalline ſtreams. The winds are partial to this peaceful grove, and none but gentle zephyrs whiſper thro' her trees. There the nymphs and fauns by night aſſemble, and whilſt *Pan* plays on his melodious pipe, ſtrike with their feet alternately the ground. So thick, ſo interwoven are the trees, no ſun-beams e'er can pierce them. There ſolemn ſilence reigns and peaceful gloom; there, night and day, ſoft breezes fan the woods. Amidſt the trembling leaves ſad *Philomela* ſits, and tells her mournful tale; ſings all the night; but ſings, alas! in vain. Upon another ſpray, a LINNET warbling ſings, and with her cheerful notes proclaims to all the neighbouring ſwains the approach of ſpring. So ſweet ſhe ſang, the Nightingale herſelf grew jealous. One day they ſpied a ſwain, within the center of the grove, whom they had never ſeen before. They gazed on him with pleaſure, and took him for ſome noble youth, a lover of the Muſes and of Muſic. They fancied he might be *Apollo* in diſguiſe, as once he was when ſhepherd to *Admetus*, or at leaſt ſome hero to the Gods allied. The birds, by inſpiration of the Muſes, thus began their tuneful ſong in concert.

Who is this ſhepherd, or this God unknown, who honours thus our grove? He liſtens to our harmleſs notes with pleaſure. The Muſes are, we find, his favourites : their melting founds will tune his generous foul, and make him lovely as he's great.

Then *Philomel* purfued the fong alone.

O ! may our Hero's virtues multiply, like the gay flowers in spring ! May he delight in innocent and rational amufements ! May the foft Graces hang on his lips, and wife Minerva *dwell within his heart.*

The LINNET then replied.

O ! may the mufic of his tongue prove more melodious than the lyre of Orpheus ! *May he in time to come be more renowned for his heroic actions than* Alcides ! *May he be more couragious, but not fo rafh, and fo unguarded as* Achilles ! *May he be good and wife, love all mankind, and be by them beloved ! And may the Mufes tune his foul to every virtue !*

Then the infpired birds again in chorus joined.

Our tuneful notes charm his attentive ears, and fink into his heart, as gentle dews into the thirfly earth. May the gracious Gods incline his heart to mercy, and make him ever happy ! May his hand ever grafp the horn of plenty, and thro' his means the golden age return ! May his good conduct influence all mankind, and flowers forever fpring up where he treads !

Whilft thus the feathered chorifters their defcants fang, the zephyrs, loth to interrupt their mufic, dropt their wings. The various parti-coloured flowers that then adorned the grove reared up their cheerful heads. The ftreams, which the three *Naïades* poured from their noify urns crept filently along. The fauns and fatyrs with ears erect, liftened attentive to their charming founds. Echo, well-pleafed, repeated every note to all the concave rocks. A long train of *Dryads* iffued from their hollow trunks to gaze with admiration on the godlike youth, for whofe fuccefs fweet *Philomela* and the warbling *Linnet* thus zealoufly in concert joined their wifhes.

FABLE

F A B L E XIII.

The D R A G O N and two F O X E S.

ONce on a time, a DRAGON fat brooding over an immenfe
treafure, and to fecure it, never clofed his eyes to reft.
Two FOXES, well verfed in every fly mercurial art, infinuated themfelves into his favor by fulfome flattery and adulating addrefs. He
entertained them as his friends and confidents. We ought always
to be jealous of men's forward proteftations : an artful complaifance
too often flows from a perfidious heart. They pay their court to
him as to a King, applaud all his fchemes, tho' never fo ridiculous;
give into his fentiments, tho' moft apparently unjuft, and knowing
his foible, turn and wind him at their pleafure. In full confidence
of thefe two bofom-friends, he ventured to take an hour's repofe ;
but as foon as the credulous fool fell faft afleep, they ftrangled him,
and feized the glorious prize. Their next bufinefs was to divide
the plunder fairly between them ; an affair not eafily accomplifhed ;
for villains feldom can agree in any point, but the bare execution of
their crimes. One of thefe hypocrites, with a philofophic air addreffed
his companion. Brother, fays he, of what fervice is all this hoard of
gold to us ? A hare, or a rabbit, had been a better booty. Thefe fame
guineas will prove but a poor meal. We have not ftomachs, like the
oftrich, to digeft them. What fools men are to make this gold their
God ? Brother, let us be wifer. The other with equal hypocrify replied;
your obfervations are ftrictly juft, brother, and I'll affure you, they
have made a convert of me : I am now fully convinced, that the
philofopher is the happy man ; and for the future, like *Bias* of old,

I'll

I'll carry all I have about me. Both affected to depart from the ill-gotten, worthlefs treafure without reluctance : both lay in ambufcade ; and confcious of their mutual guilt, deftroyed each other. One, as he lay expiring, thus addreffed his dying partner : what would you have done with all that gold had you fuccceded? The fame, replied the other, as you propofed, had fortune favoured you. By accident a paffenger going by, and enquiring into the fatal caufe of their difafter, declared they were both fools. Fools as we are, fays one of them, you men are juft the fame: Gold is no more food for you than us, and yet you'll cut your brother's throat for gain. Before this unhappy accident, our prudent race defpifed the fatal charm. That, which you introduced for the conveniency of life, is now become its greateft torment, You fly from true felicity, in fearch after an imaginary good.

F A B L E

FABLE XIV.

The Two FOXES.

TWO Foxes contrived one night by ftratagem to plunder a hen-rooft. The cock, the hen and chickens, fell an eafy facrifice to their fuperior power. After this bloody conqueft, the victors fupped upon the fpoil. One of them, that was young, and a perfect epicure, propofed to eat them all at once. The other, that was old and avaricious, thought it much more prudent to preferve fome part againft a time of need. Dear child, faid he, experience has made me wife. I have feen the world, and the viciffitudes of fortune. Let us not be fo lavifh as to fpend our fubftance all at once. We have had good fuccefs; we have found a valuable treafure; and let us improve it to the beft advantage. Don't preach to me, fays the young one; for my part, I'll live here while I may; indulge my noble appetite, and lay in provifion for a week. They'll flink, you old fool, to-morrow. 'Tis nonfenfe to talk of our return: the farmer, fhould he catch us, would, no doubt, revenge their caufe, and murder us, as we have them. After this pert reply, each acted according to the dictates of his inclination. The young one indulged himfelf fo long, that he almoft burft his belly, and with much difficulty crawled into his kennel, where in a few hours he died. The old one, who had more conduct, and a greater command of his paffions, returning to his hoard the next morning, was way-laid, and fell a victim to the countryman's refentment.—Thus every age is prone to its own darling vice.—The young are wild and boundlefs in their pleafures;—the old avaricious, and incorrigibly fo to the laft.

FABLE

FABLE XV.

The WOLF and the LAMB.

A Flock of sheep were safely grazing in an enclosed meadow; the dogs were all asleep, and their master, with some fellow-swains, sat playing on their tuneful pipes beneath a shady elm. A WOLF, with hunger pinched, peeped thro' the hedge, and with a wishful eye surveyed the flock. An unexperienced thoughtless LAMB approached him. What, sir, said he to the voracious stranger, is it you want within our pasture? To taste your tender, flowery grass, replied the WOLF. What can be more delicious, than to graze as you do on the verdant meads, enamelled round with flowers, and slake one's thirst in the transparent rills? Here, I perceive, you live in perfect plenty. For my part, my ambition would rise no higher: I've learned by philosophic rules to live contented with a little. Say you so, said the LAMB, have you no appetite for flesh, and will a little grass suffice you? I find, you have been misrepresented; let us live sociably, and graze together. Immediately the LAMB leaps o'er the fence. As soon the grave philosopher turns tyrant, and tears him limb from limb. Always suspect the sincerity of such as with studied expressions applaud their own virtues. Eloquence may betray you. Let actions speak the man.

FABLE

FABLE XVI.

The CAT and the RABBITS.

ONE day a CAT, with an affected, modest air, traversed a warren, plentifully stocked with BUCKS and DOES. The whole republic trembled at the fight of him, and plunged into their burrows. As this stranger, with a fly imperious eye, stood peering at the mouth of one of their recesses; the states, who with terror had observed his dreadful claws, ordered their deputies, at their most narrow avenue, to parly with him, and demand the cause of his arrival. *Grimalkin*, in a soft, friendly tone, protested his design was innocent; that all his aim was to inform himself of the laws of their republic : that, as he made philosophy his study, he determined to travel round the globe purely to gratify his curiosity, and learn the various customs of the brutal world. The unguarded, credulous deputies, immediately made the following report to their lords and masters; that this stranger, whose modest deportment and majestic dress commanded their respect, was a sober, harmless pacific philosopher; that he was travelling thro' various kingdoms for the cultivation of his mind; that he had seen a thousand curiosities in foreign parts; that his conversation was extremely entertaining; that there was no danger of his destroying any of their young ones; that he was, in short, one of *Bramin*s disciples; that the metempsychosis was an article of his faith, and flesh his utter aversion. The grand assembly were charmed with this eloquent harangue. A sage, old BUCK, who had long been their speaker,

was juftly jealous of this grave philofopher, and offered many fubftantial reafons to juftify his fufpicions, but to no purpofe. Notwithftanding all his wife precautions, they went in a body to pay
their compliments in the moft folemn manner, to this great *Brami-*
nift, who, at their firft approach, feized feven or eight, and flew
them on the fpot. The reft, with much difficulty and confufion,
recovered their burrows, but hung down their heads, afhamed of
their credulity. Soon after this tyrannic infult, the CAT returned
to the mouth of the burrow, where he parlied with them firft, and
there made the largeft proteftations of his unfeigned forrow and
repentance : he alledged that fatal neceffity, and not choice, had
compelled him to fuch an act of hoftility ; and affured them, that
for the future he'd live contented with meaner diet, and fhould
think himfelf happy, if they'd forgive this firft tranfgreffion, and
for the future live in peace. The republic thought proper to accept of his contrition ; but determined to expofe themfelves as
little as poffible to his arbitrary power. They fign the treaty, and
pay him homage at a diftance. In the mean time, one of the boldeft
and moft active BUCKS fteps flyly out at a back-door, to a
neighb'ring fhepherd,—who delighted to captivate the young ones,
as they munched the juniper berries—relates their whole adventure.
The fwain refenting the tyrannical proceedings of the CAT, haftens
with his bow and arrows to the warren. He found the CAT attentive on his prey. Unfeen, a fatal fhaft flew to his breaft. The
tyrant, as he lay expiring, fighed out this juft reflection. The Hy-
pocrite, when once difcovered is believed no more : he is forever
hated, ever feared ; and is at laft by his own ftratagems betrayed.

F A B L E

FABLE XVII.

The MICIAN TRAVELLERS.

A MOUSE that lived forever reftlefs and uneafy, forever tormented with frightful apprehenfions of the Cat, and her deftructive party, one day called to a bofom-friend, who lodged within a hole contiguous to her own, and thus addreffed her. Neighbour, faid fhe, I have a project in my head. As I was at breakfaft one morning in a curious library, I turned over a certain book of travels, and caft my eye on a very remarkable paffage. There is a beautiful country, fays my author, called the *Indies*, where the mician race are treated with much more gentlenefs, and live much freer from infults and oppreffion than we do here. In that country 'tis the received opinion of the Sophi, that the foul of a moufe may poffibly have been the foul of a minifter of ftate, an archbifhop, or a king; and afterwards by tranfmigration, animate fome fuperior beauty, fome lady of the firft diftinction. To the beft of my remembrance, he calls this the metempfychofis. This being an eftablifhed maxim amongft them, they treat every fpecies of the brutal world with abundance of indulgence and good will. Hofpitals are there erected for the reception of the mician race: they have an annual penfion, and a table allowed them, like perfons of diftinction. Let us try our fortune, neighbour; fet fail for thefe happy iflands, where their laws are fo refined; and merit meets with fuch a due regard. But, neighbour, replied her companion, are there no Cats in thofe hofpitals you fpeak of?—If there fhould, I fancy that fame metempfychofis, as you call it, would be a

practice

practice much in vogue there, and by fome unlucky fqueeze or another, we foon fhould change our forms, and become heroes or monarchs, perhaps againft our inclinations. Never fear, fays the firft, they are ftrictly regular in all their œconomy: the cats have their feparate apartments as we have ours: they have another hofpital of invalids erected at a proper diftance. This important objection thus removed, our two MICE determined on their voyage; and by the help of a cable, which was lafhed to the fhore, got on board a veffel, the night before they weighed anchor, bound for the *Indian* coaft. Away they fail; the winds prove propitious: with tranfport they traverfe the ocean, and take their farewel of an ifland, where cats rule with fuch tyrannic fway. They had a fafe and fpeedy paffage. They landed at *Surat,* not like merchants, with a view of advantageous commerce; but in hopes to find a courteous reception from the natives. No fooner were they fettled as they propofed in one of the mician apartments, but they proudly affumed a fuperiority over the reft, and laid claim to the beft places in the houfe. The firft pretended fhe had been a celebrated *Bramin* on the coaft of *Malabar.* The other infifted, that fhe had been a celebrated toaft there, and admired for her ears that almoft touched the ground. In fhort, they were both fo faucy and imperious, that the *Indian* Mice no longer would endure their pride and infolence. A civil war immediately enfued. They unanimoufly oppofed thefe two conceited upftarts. Inftead of becoming a prey to their common foe the cat, they fell a bloody facrifice to the refentment of their own fraternity. 'Tis to little purpofe to fly for refuge into foreign countries: without a modeft and prudent deportment. We only take a deal of pains to be unhappy: misfortunes can but attend us nearer home.

F A B L E

FABLE XVIII.

The BEASTS assembled to elect a KING.

NO sooner was the Lion dead, but beasts of all denominations flocked to his den, and courtiers-like, condoled with the Lionefs, his royal relict, who made the forests, and the distant mountains tremble with her awful roaring. After the usual compliments they proceeded to a new election. The crown of the deceased was, with all due solemnity and decorum, placed in the midst of the august assembly. His royal offspring was too feeble and too young to sieze the crown, to which so many much more powerful creatures laid their claim. Give me but time to grow a little, says the royal cub, and in a few years you shall find I can fill the throne, and make the world around me tremble, as my father did before me. In the mean time, I'll practife the heroic actions of my ancestors, and one day equal them in glory. The crown I challenge, says the Leopard, as my regal right. My person is the nearest representative of his late majesty deceased. As for my part, says Bruin, I insist upon it: 'tis an act of injustice to prefer the Leopard before me. I boast an equal strength; am as couragious, and as blood-thirsty as he; add to this—an advantage of no small importance—my art of climbing trees: I appeal, says the Elephant, to the whole assembly here present, whether any one, with justice, can pretend to be so big, so strong, or so sedate as I am. I am the noblest, the most beautifully formed of all the brutal world, replied the Horse. I the most politic, strait Reynard
cried.

cried. Who's fwifter, faid the Stag, than I ? Where, faid the Monkey, can you find a king fo gay, fo entertaining as myfelf ? my
actions would be ever pleafing to my loving fubjects. Befides, who
is fo near allied to man, the lord of the creation ? The Parrot in-
terpofed, and made his fpeech. I think, fir, I can boaft that right
with a much better grace than you. Your frightful phiz, I own,
and antic poftures faintly refemble his. I boaft a nobler faculty :
I imitate his fpeech, the demonftration of his reafon, and his greateft glory. Pert fool, replied the Monkey, hold your peace. You
talk 'tis true, but not like man. You chatter only a fet form of
words ; not one you underftand. Thefe two egregious copiers of
mankind made all the affembly fmile. At laft, after a long debate,
the Elephant was crowned their king elect : he had, they owned,
fufficient ftrength and conduct to protect them : abhorred the arbitrary power of beafts of prey, and never was fo idly vain, fo felf-
conceited, as to pretend to be what, in reality, he was not.

FABLE XIX.

The MONKEY.

AN arch, old MONKEY having departed this life, his ghoft defcended to the infernal regions, and there petitioned *Pluto* for his indulgence to return to earth. The God confented he fhould animate the dull, inactive Afs, to cure him of his thoufand little, fprightly, fly, unlucky pranks. But the gay, comic ghoft performed his wanton fopperies with fuch fuccefs before him, that the grim monarch laughed aloud, and granted what he afked without reftriction. With your majefty's permiffion then, I'll now inform the Parrot. By this tranfmigration, faid he, I fhall at leaft retain fome faint refemblance of mankind, whofe actions I fo long have copied. When a Monkey, their geftures were the objects of my imitation ; when a Parrot, I fhall mimick their difcourfe. No fooner had the Monkey's foul informed the Parrot, but a filly, tatling, fuperannuated lady purchafed him. He was the darling of her heart, and honoured with a curious cage. His fare was uncommonly delicious, and he prattled all day long with the old dotard, whofe difcourfe was as nonfenfical as his. To this new noify faculty, he fubjoined I know not what of his old little affectations. His head was in perpetual motion. His bill cracked ; his wings fluttered ; and his feet were thrown into a thoufand ridiculous poftures. His old miftrefs would, ever and anon, mount her fpectacles upon her nofe to peer at her favourite bird. She would often lament, that her ears were fomewhat defective, by
which

which misfortune she too often loft the beauty of poor Poll's expreffions, which she imagined were ever witty and refined. The
Parrot, by this exceffive indulgence, grew loud, impertinent and
foolish. In short, he was so reftlefs, so wanton in his cage, and
fipped cordial waters so plentifully with his old lady, that once more
he died. His ghoft making now its second appearance before the
throne of *Pluto*, the God refolved to tongue-tie him forever, and
doomed him to animate a fish: but when the gloomy monarch
faw again his comical grimaces, he revoked the fentence. Princes
fometimes favour fools and parafites. The ghoft is a fecond time
indulged, and fuffered to inform a man. But as the God had fome
regard for virtue, he carefully confined him to the body of a noify,
impertinent tongue-pad; a fellow, that was forever venting im-
probable ftories; a felf-conceited coxcomb; an unnatural mimic;
a fnarling, injudicious critic; one, in short, that would interrupt
the moft refined converfation, to hear himfelf talk, and introduce
his own nonfenfical difcourfe. *Mercury*, who recollected him, tho'
so difguifed, thus with a fmile addreffed him. Thou fool, I know
thee well enough. I've feen thee long e'er now. Thou worthlefs
compound of the Ape and Parrot! Take but away thy antic geftures,
and a few hard terms, which thou haft learnt by rote, but canft
not underftand, and thou haft nothing left. A pretty Parrot and a
fprightly Monkey, when compounded, make but one filly coxcomb.
Alas! what numbers are there in the town, who by their artful
cringes, ftudied addreffes, and affected airs, without one grain of
wifdom are careffed, and thought men of vaft importance?

FABLE XX.

The two Young LIONS.

TWO young LIONS had been reared together in one foreft. Their ftature, ftrength and age were equal. One was taken captive by the Great Mogul. The other ranged, without reftraint, amongft the craggy mountains. The firft was by the huntfmen ftrait conveyed to court, where long he lived in luxury and eafe. He feldom dined without an antelope, or e'er repofed but on a bed of down. A fair eunuch conftantly attended twice a day, to comb his graceful golden main. When he was polifhed and made tractable, the monarch would himfelf carefs him. He foon grew plump, fmooth, comely and majeftic. A golden collar graced his neck; diamonds and pearls adorned his ears. He looked with an eye of contempt on his brother-lions, who inhabited the dens adjacent; they were not equal favourites with him; nor their apartments fo commodious or well-furnifhed as his own. His grandeur and fuccefs with pride elate his heart; he vainly thinks the favours that he meets with, the refult of merit. His court-education fired his mind with falfe ambition. He imagined, that had he ranged the foreft unconfined, by this time he had been fome mighty hero. One day, he quits the court, and travels, big with expectation, to his native country. At the fame juncture his old royal mafter died; and the ftates were all affembled, to fill by vote the vacant throne. Among the numerous candidates, there appeared one much fterner and much more

imperious

imperious than the reſt. This lordly, dauntleſs hero was our gay
courtier's old companion, who had never been a ſlave. Whilſt
the one had been indulged in all the luxury and pride of courts;
the other, urged by the pure appetite of nature, was often exer-
ciſed in dreadful combats, and ſcorned all dangers for a bare ſub-
ſiſtance. Shepherds as well as flocks fell victims to his fury. His
carcaſe was both lean and ſhaggy; ghaſtly were his looks. His
eyes were bloodſhot, and ſeemed all on fire. His limbs were ſtrong
and active; he could climb the trees, and ſpring upon his prey,
fearleſs of darts or jav'lins. Theſe two old companions propoſed
to the auguſt aſſembly to decide their right by ſingle combat. But
an old, ſage, experienced Lioneſs, to whoſe judgment the whole
body paid peculiar deference, perſuaded them to fix upon the
throne, without delay, the politician that was bred at court.
There were ſeveral mal-contents on this advice: they murmured,
that an effeminate, luxurious prince ſhould be preferred ; whilſt the
bold warrior, long inured to toils, fearleſs of dangers, and well
able to ſupport his cauſe, ſhould be neglected. However, the old
Lioneſs, by her ſuperior influence, huſhed the riſing ſtorm, and
fixed the courtier on the throne. At his firſt acceſſion to the
crown he revelled in delight; indulged himſelf in luxury and eaſe;
by artifice and ſmooth addreſs, concealed his innate fury, and his
love of lawleſs power. His ſubjects ſoon neglected, ſcorned, de-
teſted him. Now, ſays the old Lioneſs, 'tis proper to dethrone
him. I foreknew his want of merit; but was deſirous you ſhould
have a monarch for a while, bred up and ſpoiled in a luxurious
court, that you might learn to value courage, conduct and true
merit, where you found it. Now is the time to let them fight or
die. The two heroes were immediately conducted into a large
encloſure, and the aſſembly, big with expectations, gazed at the
gallant ſhow, a ſhow, that ſoon was over. The courtier trembled

at

at his foe, and durſt not once approach him. He fled, and ſtrove
to be concealed. The foreſter purſued, and called him with diſ-
dain a coward. All the ſpectators cried; tear him in pieces.
Have no mercy on the poor poltroon. No, no, replied the victor,
when a coward is a foe, 'tis cowardice indeed to be afraid. Let
him ſtill live. Death, from my hands, would be too great an
honour. I ſhall know how to reign, and keep him ever in ſub-
jection without danger. In ſhort, the dauntleſs Lion ruled his
ſubjects with the wiſdom and good conduct of *Minerva*. The
other was content to cringe, and creep, and fawn for trivial favours;
and ſpent the poor remainder of his days, in ſhameful and inglo-
rious eaſe.

F A B L E

FABLE XXI.

The BEES.

ONE day, when gentle zephyrs fanned the air, and nature was arrayed in all her glory, a young, gay Prince was walking in a curious garden. All on a sudden, an unusual found invades his ears; he turns about, and at a distance sees a bee-hive. The novelty induced him to approach it. With pleasure and amazement he observed the industry, the conduct and œconomy of that republic. Their cells were very visible, and regularly formed. One party was employed to fill those cellars with nectar. Others brought in their store of flowers, collected from the bosom of the spring. In this republic none lived in indolence and ease. Every one was full employed; but no one hurried, or confounded. Those at the helm, directed the inferiors, who laboured all the day, without a murmur, or the least reflection. As their exact obedience was the peculiar object of the Prince's admiration. A Bee, whom all the commonwealth acknowledged as supreme, with graceful air approached, and thus addressed him. The œconomy, which you observe amongst us, has been, I find, an amusement to you: but make it rather, royal Sir, a lesson of instruction. No factious fools, no lawless libertines, are known amongst us. No one expects our favour and indulgence; but he, who labours hard, and studies to promote the public good. True merit is the only claim to posts of trust. We study night and day to be of service to mankind. O! may I live to hail the day, when you shall copy us, and rule mankind by laws as just as ours!

FABLE

FABLE XXII.

The B E E and the F L Y.

ONE day a BEE obferved a FLY, that fettled, as fhe thought,
too near her hive. In an imperious tone, fhe cried, what is
thy bufinefs ? How durft thou, faucy thing, approach us regents of
the air ? The FLY, ironically, with a fmile, replied; amazing infolence ! wonderful prefumption truly ! How groundlefs is your
refentment ? You are a race of fuch peevifh, ill-natured, unfociable
creatures, that none but fools would e'er regard you. No nation
under the fun, replied the BEE, has that good conduct and œconomy
as we have. Our laws are all peculiar to ourfelves, and our republic
is the wonder of the world. We trade in nothing but celeftial honey, a liquor as delicious as the nectar of the Gods. Out of my
fight, thou faucy, worthlefs wretch, whofe every meal's offenfive.
The FLY replied, we make our lives as eafy as we can : adverfity's
no crime, tho' paffion is. Your honey, I allow, is to perfection pure ;
but your proud hearts are wretchedly polluted. Your laws with
juftice all admire. But then your conftitutions are too warm : you
all take fire too foon. You'll facrifice your lives to gratify the leaft
refentment. 'Tis better to be modeft and good-natured, than haughty
and imperious, and have fo nice a tafte for mere punctilios.

FABLE

FABLE XXIII.

The BEES and the SILK-WORMS.

ONE day the Bees foared up as high as the throne of *Jupiter*, fell proftrate at his feet, and with fubmiffion hoped for his indulgence, in return for their good offices of old, their former care of him when a helplefs infant on *Mount Ida*. *Jove* gracioufly accepted their addrefs, and thought it was juft to grant them the precedence to all other infects: but *Minerva*, who prefides o'er all the arts and fciences, informed him, that there was another race as beneficial to mankind as they.—Their names, fays *Jove*.—The Goddefs anfwered him, the Silk-Worms—forthwith, the God commiffioned *Mercury* to fummon all their deputies, and ordered proper zephyrs to attend him, who fhould waft them on their gentle wings to high *Olympus*, that he himfelf might hear what the contending parties had to offer. The ambaffadrefs from the republic of the Bees opened the folemn caufe; enlarged upon the fweetnefs of their honey, the nectar of mankind, its various virtues, and its artful compofition; from thence proceeded to the wifdom of their laws, and the exact œconomy of their republic. We, continued the female orator, and we alone can boaft the honour of fupporting the great father of the Gods, when, in a cave expofed, a tender, helplefs infant. Moreover, our courage in the field is equal to our induftry at home; let but our royal leader bid us charge the foe, we bravely fight or die. Invincible affurance ! How could thefe Worms, thefe abject,

L

worthlefs

worthlefs infects, think to difpute this point with us? Infects, that only grovel upon earth; whilft we have nobler powers; with golden wings can mount the azure fkies. To this the advocate for the Silk-Worms modeftly replied. We readily acknowledge that we are but reptiles; that we cannot boaft that courage and good conduct which our antagonifts moft juftly can. However, each individual member of our ftate is a meer prodigy in nature, and for the public good confumes his very vitals. Tho' lawlefs, ftill we live in peace. No civil difcords e'er diftract our ftate, to which the factious Bees are ever fubject. Like *Proteus* we are ever changing, and tho' our form's but fmall, we boaft eleven, gay, parti-coloured ringlets, beauteous as the bow of *Iris*, or the moft artificial flower. Our labours grace the monarch on the throne; nay more, they help to furnifh the gay temples of the Gods. Our manufacture's beautiful and lafting; not like their honey, which, tho' fweet whilft new, is very fubject to decay. In fhort, we transform ourfelves to little Beans; but Beans, that have a grateful fmell; that ftill retain their motion, and the figns of life. At laft, we metamorphofe into gaudy Butterflies. Then are our forms more beauteous than the bees; then we can boaft as bold a flight tow'rds Heaven as they. I've nothing more to offer, but fubmit to *Jove*. The God was at a lofs to give his final judgment in fo nice a caufe; at laft, however, he declared in favour of the Bees; fince cuftom time out of mind confirmed their right. How ungrateful fhould I be, *Jove* added in excufe, fhould I degrade my friends, who ferved me in diftrefs. No, I'll ever own the favour. However, ftill, in my private opinion, mankind have greater obligations to the Silk-Worms.

F A B L E

F A B L E XXIV.

The Conceited O W L.

A Young. Owl, who, *Narciſſus*-like, had ſurveyed himſelf
with pleaſure in a chryſtal ſtream, and thought himſelf, not
only fairer than the light, for *Phœbus* is no deity of his, but fair
as Night herſelf, his favourite Goddeſs, thus began his proud ſo-
liloquy. How often have I offered incenſe to the Graces! When
I was born, fair *Cytharea* dreſt me in her ceſtos. Young ſmiling
cupids fan their wanton wings around me. I'm now of age ;
Hymen ſhall bleſs me with a numerous iſſue, beauteous as myſelf :
they ſhall in time become the glory of the groves, the darlings of
the night! O! ſhould the race of Owls be once extinct, the loſs
would be irreparable. Thrice happy muſt that fair one be, that
ſhall be circled in my arms! Fired with theſe ſelf-conceited
thoughts, he ſends the Crow to the dread monarch of the birds
with bold propoſals of a match between himſelf and his fair
daughter, the royal Eaglet. Fain would the Crow have been
excuſed from this commiſſion. What reception can I expect,
ſaid ſhe, in the propoſal of a match ſo viſibly unequal ? How can
you imagine, that the Eaglet, who can, unhurt, gaze ſtedfaſt on
the ſun, ſhould wed with you, whoſe tender eyes can't bear the
dawn of day ? Light and darkneſs can never poſſibly agree. You'd
live forever in a ſtate of ſeparation. The ſelf-conceited Owl was
deaf to all advice. The Crow, to ſooth his vanity, complied at
laſt, and made the propoſition. They ſmiled at the ridiculous

requeſt.

requeſt.   However, the monarch anſwered ; if your maſter be
ambitious of my favour,   let him meet me in the regions of the air
to-morrow about mid-day.   The proud ambitious fool attempts the
flight.   All on a ſudden a dim ſuffuſion veiled his eyes, unable to
endure the radiant light, downwards he ſunk upon a rock.   All the
feathered race purſued, and ſtript him of his plumes.   A cavern
now he finds his greateſt happineſs, and he reſolves to wed an Owl,
an humble tenant of the rock.   The nuptials were conſummated at
night ;   and as they both were blind, they thought each other fair.
Pride will have its fall.   We ſhould not aim to ſhine in ſpheres we
cannot poſſibly adorn.

FABLE XXV.

CLEOBULUS and PHILLIS.

A Penſive ſhepherd once led his flock to paſture on the flow'ry banks of the river *Achelöus*. The Fauns and Satyrs, that lay concealed in the adjacent groves, danced on the verdant graſs to his melodious pipe. The water-nymphs, ſporting beneath the waves, advanced amidſt the ruſhes, attentive to his charming muſic. *Achelöus* too, reclining on his urn, reared up his head, which, ſince his combat with the mighty *Hercules*, had loſt a horn, and the harmonious ſounds ſuſpended for a time the tortures of the vanquiſhed God. The admiring Naiades made no impreſſion on the ſwain: PHILLIS alone was the dear object of his wiſhes ; PHILLIS, the plain, the modeſt nymph, the beauty unadorned ; who never ſhone with borrowed rays ; contented with thoſe charms alone the Graces gave her. PHILLIS went from home into the meadows, thoughtful of nothing but her tender flock, herſelf alone inſenſible of all her charms ; the neighb'ring nymphs grew jealous: The ſwain adored her, but wanted courage to declare his paſſion. Her ſevere virtue and unaffected modeſty, thoſe never-dying charms of beauty, that awed her lovers, and kept them at a diſtance, were the chief objects of his admiration ; but *Cupid* is a ſubtle God ; a thouſand little arts he ſoon invents that ſhall reveal the ſecret. The ſhepherd ſoon concluded the pleaſing, tho' unſtudied ſong he had begun, to introduce another, more artificial, that might melt his charmer down to love. He knew her taſte ; that ſhe admired ſtories of

heroic

heroic virtue. He fung, therefore, under a fictitious name, his own adventures; for in thofe days heroes themfelves were fhepherds, and condefcended to their drefs. Thus then he began his martial fong. When *Polynices* went to the fiege of *Thebes*, in hopes to dethrone his brother *Eteocles*, all the Grecian powers efpoufed his caufe, and armed in their chariots, lay before the city. Here *Adroftus*, father-in-law to the great *Polynices*, with fury urged the war: Thoufands fell victims to his fword; as the yellow harveft bends beneath the fickle. There *Amphiaräus*, the celebrated forcerer, who had foretold his own untimely fate, mingled amongft the crowd, when, on a fudden, the earth gaped wide, and fwallowed him to quick deftruction. As he was tumbling down the dark abyfs, he curft his planet, and his day of marriage. At fome fmall diftance, the two fons of *Oedipus* were clofe engaged in dreadful combat. As the Leopard and the Tyger, when they meet upon the rocks of *Caucafus*, with inbred fury contend for victory; fo thefe irreconcileable heroes fought rolling upon the ground, refolved to die or conquer. During this unnatural engagement *Cleobulus*, an attendant on *Polynices*, oppofed a mighty *Theban*, a favourite of *Mars*. The arrow, which the *Theban* threw, directed by the God himfelf, had fealed the fate of young CLEOBULUS, had he not, with incredible activity, fprung from the deadly blow. CLEOBULUS, in a moment, turned upon the *Theban*, and with his jav'lin ftruck him to the heart. The reeking blood gufhed from the gaping wound; his eyes grew dim and languifhing; his foul lay ftruggling to be loofed, and death foon caft his fable veil o'er all his manly features. Soon as the dear partner of his bed difcerned from a high tower her hufband's fall, her lovely eyes were drowned in floods of forrow. Thrice happy foldier, tho' thus vanquifhed to be fo pitied, and fo well beloved! With how much tranfport could I yield to fate on fuch conditions! What is youth, what is beauty, and a thirft for fame,

if

if the fair nymph, the object of our wishes, still difdains us ? Phillis, who liftened with attention to his charming fong, was now
convinced, the fhepherd was himfelf Cleobulus, that flew the
Theban. His conqueft now began to fire her heart ; fhe views his
beauties with a lover's eye, and pities all his pains. The fair now
gives her hand, and plights her faith. In a few days, *Hymen* confirmed their joys. The neighb'ring fwains, the rural Deities themfelves, with envious eyes, behold the happy pair. They lived together to a good old age, and fpent their days, like the famed
Baucis and *Philemon,* in rural fports, in innocence and love.

F A B L E

FABLE XXVI.

CHROMIS and MNASYLUS.

CHROMIS.

HOW cool this grotto is! What ſtately trees! How thick and verdant are the leaves! How gloomy are the walks! How ſweetly *Philomela* tells her mournful tale!

MNASYLUS.

True, theſe are charms; but there are nobler objects ſtill in view.

CHROMIS.

What! thoſe ſtatues do you mean? For my part, I can ſee no beauty in them. How unpoliſhed that firſt figure ſeems to be!

MNASYLUS.

'Tis the image of a beauty for all that. But no more on that topic. For a brother-ſwain, you know, has ſaid all that can poſſibly be offered in its commendation.

CHROMIS:

Then you mean that ſhepherdeſs, I preſume, that bends over the fountain.

MNASYLUS.

No, no, nor that. Our *Lycidas* has tuned her praiſes on his rural pipe; and who ſhall after him preſume to ſing?

CHROMIS.

Then you muſt certainly mean that young figure in the corner.

MNASYLUS.

M N A S Y L U S.

I do fo.—If you obferve, it has not that rural air as the other two have.—'Tis a Goddefs, you muft know. *Pomona,* or one of her attendants at leaft : in her right hand, fhe grafps a cornucopiæ, filled with autumnal fruits ; in her left an urn, from whence, with a profufe hand, fhe fcatters gold ; poffeffed at once of the gay products of the earth, the wealth of nature, and thofe richer treafures which mankind adore.

C H R O M I S.

How fhe declines her head ! — Is that an artful pofture ?

M N A S Y L U S.

Yes :—for all ftatues, if elevated high, to be furveyed below, ftand in the faireft point of light, when they incline.

C H R O M I S.

But is not that head-drefs fomething particular? None of our modern beauties ever drefs fo.

M N A S Y L U S.

That may be ; but the air is very carelefs and becoming notwithftanding. How curioufly fome hairs are parted all before !—How gracefully fome locks hang curling on each fide ; whilft a gay riband binds the reft behind !

C H R O M I S.

Your opinion of the drapery.—Why, pray, fo many folds ?

M N A S Y L U S.

Oh !—'tis à-la-negligée.—A girdle, you fee, tucks up her gown, that fhe may trace the grove with greater freedom : the loofe, flowing drapery is much more graceful than a formal drefs.—One would almoft imagine, that the ftatuary had foftened the very marble, the plaits are fo natural.—If you obferve, there are fome parts vifibly naked thro' the veil. The foftnefs of the flefh, added to the beauty of the drapery, ftrikes the eye at once, and makes the whole a ravifhing performance.

C H R O M I S.

Ho, ho ! I find your affect tafte.—You talk like an artift.—But pray tell me, fince you are fuch a critic, was that cornucopiæ plucked by *Alcides* from the head of *Achelöus*, or was it *Amalthæa*'s, the famed nurfe of *Jove* ?

M N A S Y L U S.

That's a queftion too curious to be refolved in a moment.—Be-fides, I muft haften to my flock. Adieu !

A CHA-

A

CHARACTER.

The SELF-TORMENTOR.

WHY ſits *Melanthus* thus dejected and forlorn? No real, but imaginary ills torment him. His affairs move ſmoothly on; his friends all ſtudy to oblige him. Why then,—why puts he on this melancholy gloom? Laſt night he went to bed the darling of mankind; but when he roſe, a trifle diſcompoſed him; the morning low'red, and heavily brought on the day; all around him were in pain. Now his friends bluſh for ſhame. They muſt conceal him: his mind's all dark and gloomy, filled with imaginary fears. He ſighs, and like an infant weeps; with horror like a lion roars. A melancholy cloud darkens his underſtanding: ink is not blacker than his thought. Talk not to him of any thing he values moſt in life; for what he ſo admires is in a moment the object of his ſcorn and hatred. His boon companions, who, but the day before, were favourite friends, are now grown tedious, and he reſolves to ſhake them off forever. He ſeeks all occaſions to contradict, to make complaints, to exaſperate all about him; then frets that his reſentments don't provoke them. Sometimes, with his clinched fiſts, he beats the empty air; as, with his goring horns,

the bull runs furious, and combats with the winds. When he
wants a proper opportunity to rail at other, he directs his difcourfe
to himfelf, blames his own ill-conduct, calls himfelf worthlefs
coxcomb, fits down difconfolate, and takes it ill if you attempt to
pity, or redrefs him. One moment he would be alone; the next,
retirement is infupportable. He feeks his company again; again
is churlifh, and ill-natured. If they don't talk, their filence is affected and offenfive. If they whifper, he liftens with a jealous ear.
If they difcourfe too loud, they talk too much, and are too gay and
airy. If dull and penfive, he thinks it a tacit reflection on himfelf. If they laugh, he imagines that his conduct is the fubject of
their ridicule. What muft be done ?—Be as patient, as he is impertinent, and wait, in friendly hope, he'll be again to day, as prudent as he was the day before. This unaccountable humour ebbs
and flows ; when it affects him, it may properly be called the fpring
of a machine that will foon fall to pieces. Juft fo, we fhould defcribe a man, tormented with a devil ; reafon is turned the wrong
fide outward. 'Tis folly's mafter-piece. Make the experiment.
You may perfuade him that 'tis night, when the fun fhines in his
full glory ; for night and day are equally the fame to an imagination
fo ruffled and difturbed. Sometimes, he'll reflect with admiration
on his excefs of humour ; and fmile amidft his gloomy thoughts at
his egregious flights. But how fhall we prevent thefe outrages of
nature, and allay the rifing ftorm ?—It is not in the power of art.
We have no almanack extant to fettle fuch precarious weather.
Be cautious how you fay, to-morrow we'll divert ourfelves in fuch
or fuch a garden ; the man to-morrow is another creature. That
which he engages to perform one moment, is the next forgot ; 'tis
to no purpofe to remind him of his verbal promife. But inftead,
you'll

you'll find an unaccountable fomewhat, which neither has, nor can
have any proper name or form, and is impoffible to be defined, like
Proteus ever changing. Study him well ; then pafs your judgment.
In a moment he'll be the fame he was before. This fickle humour
will, and will not ; he plays the bully and the coward ; mingles
the moft favage infults with the vileft and moft low fubmiffions.
He plays the merry Andrew, weeps, fmiles, and raves ; and in thofe
fits is moft extravagant. He is diverting, florid, artificial, full of
evafions, without one ray of reafon. Never tell him he is not juft,
punctual, or a man of judgment : he'll furely take the advantage,
and retort upon you. He'll refign his folly, and refume the man of
fenfe, for the mere fatisfaction of convincing you, that you are
otherwife. Like a bubble, blown up in the air, his reafon's in a
moment loft, and never heard of more. He never knows the real
caufe of his difpleafure ; he only knows that he is, and will be dif-
pleafed ; nay, fometimes he fcarce knows even that. He imagines
oftentimes, that his friends who talk with him are warm ; whilft
he alone is cool. He's like a man afflicted with the jaundice, who
fanfies every object in his view is yellow ; tho' that colour is only
in his own eyes, and the effect of his diftemper. However, are
there no perfons whom he peculiarly regards, who are his favourite
friends ?—No ! his caprice yields to none ; all feel the effects of it
alike. He vents his paffion on the firft that comes ; friends and
foes are all the fame, in cafe he can but gratify his humour. He'll
caft his vile reflections on the very perfons to whom he lies under
the greateft obligations. He defpifes their friendfhip. They
flight him, dun him, blaft his character ; he values no man living.
Have patience but a moment, and the fcene is changed. He thinks
himfelf obliged to all mankind ; he refpects them ; they regard
him ; he fawns and flatters ; they, who before thought ill of him,

are

are charmed with his addrefs.   He freely owns his accufations all
unjuft, laughs at his follies, and acts them in ridicule all o'er again
fo naturally, you'd think him in the wildeft tranfports.   After this
farce is over, at his own expence, you might well imagine he'd
never perfonate the humourift more.—Alas! you are deceived :—
he will be mad as ever to-night in very purpofe—to laugh his folly
o'er again to-morrow.

www.ingramcontent.com/pod-product-compliance
Lightning Source LLC
Chambersburg PA
CBHW032152010726
47493CB00008BA/2674